Something kept him rooted to the spot.

There was a chance here, for redemption, for retribution, for rebirth. Salvation lay in the small, compact body of a sweet-faced four-year-old boy.

His boy.

Jameson dug deep for fortitude. "I need to be part of his life, Nina."

She hugged herself tight. "No."

"One way or another, Nina. I *will* be part of his life."

Her brown gaze narrowed. "Meaning what?"

"You can't keep him from me." His stomach churned as he forced out the words. "I have rights."

"No, you don't. I'm his mother. You're nothing to him."

"I want to be something." Desperation to make her understand moved Jameson nearer. He hated himself for the fear he saw in her face, but he couldn't back down.

"Nina…" He touched her lightly on the shoulder and she shivered. "It doesn't have to be…a conventional marriage. We can share a house, share a life, but not…"

Tears glistened in her eyes as understanding dawned on her. She could have Jameson's name but his heart was strictly off-limits.

Dear Reader,

It's that time of year again—back to school! And even if you've left your classroom days far behind you, if you're like me, September brings with it the quest for everything new, especially books! We at Silhouette Special Edition are happy to fulfill that jones, beginning with *Home on the Ranch* by Allison Leigh, another in her bestselling MEN OF THE DOUBLE-C series. Though the Buchanans and the Days had been at odds for years, a single Buchanan rancher—Cage—would do anything to help his daughter learn to walk again, including hiring the only reliable physical therapist around. Even if her last name did happen to be Day....

Next, THE PARKS EMPIRE continues with Judy Duarte's *The Rich Man's Son,* in which a wealthy Parks scion, suffering from amnesia, winds up living the country life with a single mother and her baby boy. And a man passing through town notices more than the *passing* resemblance between himself and newly adopted infant of the local diner waitress, in *The Baby They Both Loved* by Nikki Benjamin. In *A Father's Sacrifice* by Karen Sandler, a man determined to do the right thing insists that the mother of his child marry him, and finds love in the bargain. And a woman's search for the truth about her late father leads her into the arms of a handsome cowboy determined to give her the life her dad had always wanted for her, in *A Texas Tale* by Judith Lyons. Last, a man with a new face revisits the ranch—and the woman—that used to be his. Only, the woman he'd always loved was no longer alone. Now she was accompanied by a five-year-old girl...with very familiar blue eyes....

Enjoy, and come back next month for six complex and satisfying romances, all from Silhouette Special Edition!

Gail Chasan
Senior Editor

Please address questions and book requests to:
Silhouette Reader Service
U.S.: 3010 Walden Ave., P.O. Box 1325, Buffalo, NY 14269
Canadian: P.O. Box 609, Fort Erie, Ont. L2A 5X3

A Father's Sacrifice

KAREN SANDLER

Silhouette®

SPECIAL EDITION®

Published by Silhouette Books

America's Publisher of Contemporary Romance

To my father, Sam, and for his many sacrifices—
not the least of which was surviving in a household
of three crazy teenage girls. I love you, Dad!

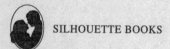

SILHOUETTE BOOKS

ISBN 0-373-24636-6

A FATHER'S SACRIFICE

Copyright © 2004 by Karen Sandler

Visit Silhouette Books at www.eHarlequin.com

Printed in U.S.A.

Books by Karen Sandler

Silhouette Special Edition

The Boss's Baby Bargain #1488
Counting on a Cowboy #1572
A Father's Sacrifice #1636

KAREN SANDLER

first caught the writing bug at age nine when, as a horse-crazy fourth grader, she wrote a poem about a pony named Tony. Many years of hard work later, she sold her first book (and she got that pony—although his name is Ben). She enjoys writing novels, short stories and screenplays and has produced two short films. She lives in Northern California with her husband of twenty-three years and two sons who are busy eating her out of house and home. You can reach Karen at karen@karensandler.net.

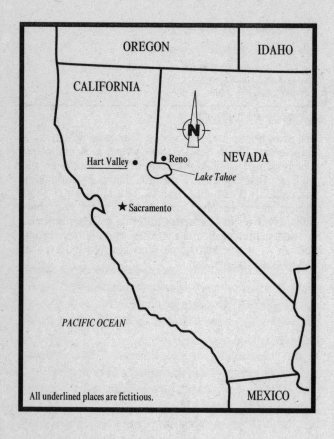

All underlined places are fictitious.

Prologue

Jameson O'Connell stared out the window of his attorney's BMW as the silver sedan wound down Prison Road toward freedom. Behind him the drab walls of Folsom Prison disappeared around a curve, vanishing from his sight.

But the memories wouldn't vanish. Those images and raw experiences would stay with him forever.

"There's a car for you," John Evans said. "I left it parked at my law office."

"A car?" Jameson glanced over at the man who had been his unexpected salvation. "Whose car?"

"Yours," John said as he pulled to a stop at the terminus of Prison Road. "A gift from your grandmother."

I don't want it! The words rose, hot and angry, in his mind, but he swallowed them back. He'd taken her money already—it had paid for the attorney's time at an astronomical hourly rate. His grandmother's wealth had paid for court costs, expert testimony, even the crisp new Dockers slacks and pristine blue polo shirt he wore.

Guilt money, all of it. But for the moment Jameson had no choice but to take it. Just as he'd had no alternative but to accept his grandmother's help in winning his release from prison.

They'd reached the Dam Road and now Folsom Lake lay to his right, green and turbulent with the scudding autumn wind. A sudden impulse sharpened within him to climb into a sailboat and ride across those choppy waters.

It hit him with as much force as a splash of Folsom's icy water—he could do it. If he wanted, he could tell John Evans to turn the damn car around and let him out. He could scout out a sailboat to rent and with his grandmother's largesse, he could climb on board and explore every one of Folsom's myriad coves. He was free—to ride a sailboat, to skip rocks on the water, to do any other fool crazy thing he wanted.

As they took the last curve on the dam, Jameson braced in his seat against the car's movement. His hands reflexively closed on the polished mahogany box in his lap.

Ridiculous really, to feel so protective of a box of ashes. But he'd never connected with his brother, Sean, while he was alive. He was loath to sever this connection with him in death.

"You have a destination in mind?" Evans asked.

Hart Valley. The answer slammed into his mind, although Jameson didn't say it aloud. The softening inside him let him know just how dangerous it was to even think of that sanctuary.

But he didn't want to think, and certainly didn't want

to make small talk with his lawyer. Evans had gotten his conviction overturned, had jumped through all the hoops on his behalf to get him set free. Jameson was grateful, truly he was. But he couldn't risk thinking of Hart Valley, because then he would think of the Russos. And if he let himself think about the Russos, his mind would inevitably wander to Nina.

And he most definitely didn't want to think about Nina.

"Not sure yet," Jameson said curtly, then pointedly turned his head to stare out the window again. Evans took the hint and fell silent.

They exchanged only the most minimal pleasantries when Evans reached his posh Granite Bay office and handed Jameson the keys to a shiny new Camry. His grandmother could have sprung for a high ticket car—a BMW like Evans's or a Mercedes. That she'd selected something more modest implied she'd given the choice some thought, had understood that he would have felt awkward and alien in a luxury vehicle.

He gripped the keys so tightly he felt them bite into his palm. Emotions gnawed at him—unwanted gratitude, a raging desire to fling the keys away, embarrassment and the overwhelming guilt that would never go away. His own, his grandmother's, Sean's.

Jameson unlocked the silver Camry and set the carved mahogany box carefully on the passenger seat. Evans handed him an envelope packed with papers laying out Sean's trust and the small fortune that now belonged to Jameson. He slid inside the car, then tossed the envelope into the foot well of the passenger seat.

He would just as soon give all his grandmother's money

away. It was blood money, money with so many strings attached he couldn't begin to undo the tangled snarl.

But as he meandered through the Sacramento streets searching for a place to go, he acknowledged that he could no more refuse his grandmother's gift than he could restore those lost four years of his life. He was a man with a bad reputation and worse history. Despite the vocational training at the prison in cabinetry, he'd be a hard sell to a prospective employer. The trust would allow him to open his own business, to give him a margin of security other recently released inmates didn't have.

He could even go up to Hart Valley, stay there if he wanted. Could make a home for himself on the scrappy five acres his late father had left him. Could set up a cabinet shop behind the derelict cabin he'd grown up in— if it was still standing after five years of neglect.

But could he face Nina?

The light at the intersection up ahead flashed from yellow to red and Jameson slammed on the brakes. The pickup in the lane behind him squealed to a halt, its front bumper nearly kissing the Camry's rear. The young hothead at the wheel of the truck shouted something profane and hit the horn the instant the light turned green again.

Jameson pulled through the intersection, regretting that he'd let Nina back inside his mind. He'd done everything he could to keep her out those four long years, reluctant to bring even her memory within those harsh gray walls of Folsom Prison. When he couldn't resist the urging of his body's heat, he blanked his mind, replaced the tempting images of Nina with one of the buxom, bland-faced pinups the other inmates plastered on their walls. He wouldn't let himself remember so much as the scent of Nina's perfume.

It all came rushing back now, though. The memories so intense, his hands shook. His grip on the Camry's wheel grew slick with sweat and he knew he'd have to pull over or risk an even closer call than the one he'd had with the pickup.

He pulled into a strip mall driveway and parked the Camry outside a discount shoe store. Sagging in his seat, he threw his head back, let his gaze wander out the side window. His chest felt tight, sharp pain digging deep. If he hadn't felt this same ache a hundred times while lying in his cell, he might have thought it was a heart attack.

You're free. You can think of her now.

He felt tears burning, but he wouldn't let them fall. Eyes squeezed shut, he released the constriction in his chest bit by bit, then let Nina in to the forbidden places.

It was dangerous, he knew, to think of her even now. But if he didn't, he thought he'd die. He needed desperately, in these few minutes of fantasy, to pretend that Nina Russo would still be the idealized woman he had held in his arms nearly five years ago. The real Nina—the one who would certainly scorn and reject him—would see through his best intentions to the dark soul beneath. So, for now, he could pretend that Nina didn't exist.

Chapter One

Nina Russo sank onto a seat at the café's counter, her feet still throbbing from the rush of the noontime crowd. Nina's Café, a Hart Valley watering hole and community meeting place, had nearly emptied as it usually did by three o'clock. The dinner rush wouldn't start up until five, and by then the night cook would be in back, ready to put up orders of meat loaf with mashed potatoes and bowls of chili.

That's if the night cook arrived on time—always a questionable proposition. Dale Zorn had not made punctuality his hallmark. In the unfortunate tradition of night cooks at Nina's, Dale had distinguished himself as being the most undependable of them all.

All but Jameson O'Connell, that is.

An odd shiver tingled up Nina's spine. What in the world had made her think of Jameson? He'd weighed heavily on her mind five years ago, both before and after that world-changing night. But since then, particularly when the town's former bad boy took a powder and left Vincent and Pauline Russo in the lurch, Nina had made it a point to keep memories of him at bay.

She was tired, that was all. Dale had been a no-show three nights out of the last seven, leaving Nina to take his place. The teenage boy she'd hired as busboy/dishwasher caught a nasty flu that had been making the rounds in Hart Valley, so she was short even that pair of hands last night.

She rubbed at her eyes and leaned back in the swivel chair with a sigh. She'd grown up in this place. She'd done her homework in the front corner booth, had played jacks on the linoleum floor while her parents finished the closing up. She'd learned every aspect of the family business, from ringing out the register to ordering the best ground beef. Key among all those lessons was the small business owner's edict—be ready to step in when someone doesn't show.

As Jameson hadn't. He'd never returned from that weekend trip to Sacramento.

Enough, she told herself. No more jaunts down memory lane. She had too much to do this afternoon to let past history haunt her.

When Lacey Mills came out from the kitchen, Nina smiled, grateful for the distraction. As willowy and tall as any fashion model, nineteen-year-old Lacey filled out her plain white waitress shirt and black slacks as if they'd been tailored for her. Nina felt the customary pang of envy that her own generous curves lacked Lacey's elegance and grace.

Lacey claimed the seat next to Nina and pushed back blond bangs. "I can stay if Dale doesn't show."

Nina shook her head, feeling her own short dark hair brush her shoulders. It was definitely time for a cut. "You've been here since six this morning. And don't you have class tonight?"

Lacey shrugged. "Yeah. But I could go straight to Marbleville from here."

A jangle up front signaled a new arrival. Nina pushed herself to her feet as she turned toward the café's door. The late autumn sunshine backlit the man entering, concealing his face with shadows. A tingle started up her back again, as if invisible fingertips grazed her spine. Nina shivered as a shred of memory teased her.

He stepped out of the shaft of sunlight, turning so it now lit his face. The harsh lines of the man's cheek and jaw, sharpened and almost gaunt with time, danced elusively in her memory. His dark brown hair was cropped close now, but she could still recall the silky feel of it. The strength of those broad shoulders suggested a remembered heat.

Then his blue eyes were riveted onto her. Pain inhabited those depths that hadn't been there five years ago, a hopelessness that made her heart ache. The hard edge to his mouth was new as well. Nina gasped as if sucker punched as full recognition burst inside her.

Lacey put a solicitous hand on her shoulder. "Nina? What's the matter?"

Nina just shook her head, trying to deny the truth that stood twenty feet away. Jameson O'Connell. He was out of prison.

Had he expected her to greet him with a smile and open arms? Jameson would have thought that hope had shriveled away within those formidable gray walls. But a tiny seed of it had remained in his heart, had fluttered to life at his first glimpse of Nina.

The sight of her horrified face should have ground hope back into oblivion, but somehow it still breathed. And that ticked him off royally, because he couldn't seem to control even that tiny speck of emotion.

He closed the distance between them, stopping just outside of arm's length, and the reality of Nina collided violently with his suppressed memories. He'd been certain he'd idealized her—given her a goddess's face, a body too lush and sensual to be real. But seeing the satiny arc of her cheek, the thick fall of black hair, her delicate chin, he could barely take a breath.

He allowed himself the briefest glance at her breasts. They were even more full than he remembered, her nipped-in waist more achingly feminine, her generous hips begging to be cupped. For just a heartbeat, he let himself recall how good it felt to draw his hands along her body, to explore each hidden curve.

Then he slammed the lid on his over-fertile imagination. Damned if he'd give temptation any more ammunition. He would have closed his eyes if he could, blocked her face from view. But if he did, he was pretty certain his heart would just stop beating.

So he kept his gaze locked with Nina's, fixed on those wide brown eyes. Briefly, he flicked a glance at her mouth, at her lips, parted slightly, then returned his focus to less perilous territory before the memory of her kiss crystallized in his mind. As he did so, a voice tugged at his attention.

"Can I help you? Would you like a table?"

Only half comprehending her query, Jameson turned to the skinny blonde sitting next to Nina. "What?"

"Can I get you a—"

Nina put one hand on the blonde's shoulder. "I'll take care of it, Lacey."

Take care of it. As if he was a chore, an unpleasant one at that. But of course he was. If Nina had a list of people she'd rather die than see again, he'd damn well top it. But that didn't change the burning in his gut.

The skinny blonde stood, hovered beside Nina. "Do you want me to—"

"Go ahead and take off," Nina said. "I've got this handled."

Her expression uncertain, the blond girl rounded the counter and grabbed a tip cup from behind it. Her gaze on Jameson, she dumped the change and bills into the pocket of her apron. "I really could—"

"Go," Nina said. "I'll see you tomorrow."

The blonde replaced her empty tip cup, then headed for the back. The quiet of the empty café seemed to close in.

Nina crossed her arms over her middle, the defensive posture framing her lush breasts in the white shirt she wore. He was grateful she hadn't starved herself into some perverse fleshless ideal, that she still possessed the soft sensuality of a woman. Then he realized the direction his thoughts had strayed and he stepped back, putting more distance between them.

She tipped her chin up. "What do you want?"

It was more challenge than question. He shoved his hands into the front pockets of his slacks and matched her tone with a question of his own. "Where are your parents?"

Her eyes narrowed. "Why the hell would I tell you that?"

He didn't like her hard edge, despaired that he had been the one to put it there. "I want to talk to them."

"About what?"

He let out an impatient puff of air, squelched the urge to tell her it was none of her damn business. "I want to thank them." The words sounded so inane verbalized.

Her mouth tightened, tugging his gaze there. "You'll have to apologize first."

The motion of her lips as she spoke mesmerized him. For an instant, his mind slid off in another direction entirely, and he had a sudden, blazingly clear memory of how her soft lips had felt pressed against the pulse at his throat.

He felt himself grow hard with just that fragment of a memory. He backed away another step, afraid that if he didn't, he'd have his hands on her in another moment.

"Nina—" He swallowed, his throat bone dry. Her name felt foreign on his tongue. "I didn't come back to cause trouble. I just want a word with your folks."

She stared at him, silent. Then she reached behind her for an order pad on the counter. "Give me your number. I'll let them know you came in."

"I don't—" he began, then remembered the cell phone Evans had given him. "Just a minute." He headed back outside to the car.

When he pulled the phone from its leather case, he was relieved to see the number printed on an adhesive tag on the back. He brought the phone into the café, and saw Nina standing exactly as he'd left her.

He read off the number and she wrote it on the pad.

She tore the top sheet off the pad and stuffed it into the pocket of her black slacks. "Excuse me, I have work to do." She started for the kitchen.

Jameson's stomach rumbled and he felt suddenly ravenous. Reflexively, he counted the hours until six o'clock, when they would have served dinner if he'd still been behind Folsom's gray walls. He'd been out three weeks, but it still hit him with the power of a revelation when he realized he didn't have to wait. He could eat now, immediately. He could order anything he wanted. He had cash in his wallet from the Prison Authority and a fistful of credit cards from the manila envelope Evans had handed him.

"I want something to eat." His words stopped her just before she disappeared into the kitchen. "Do you still have the meat loaf?"

She looked back at him, her shoulders taut with reluctance. "Yes."

"I'd like the meat loaf, then."

Resignation settled in her face. "Mashed or baked?"

His choice. The ridiculously small freedom of it swamped him. "Mashed. Extra gravy."

He didn't know what she heard in his voice, but she turned toward him and he saw something he never would have expected—sympathy and compassion. He deserved neither, but that didn't stop him from wanting them.

"Have a seat," she said. "I'll bring it out."

She continued on to the kitchen. He took a seat at the nearest booth, picked up the flatware bundled in a paper napkin. As he unwrapped the knife, fork and spoon, a sharp memory intruded—of prison meals, of the noise, the smell of bodies crowding in on him.

Before he could stop it, a familiar panic hit and along with it an overpowering urgency to escape. But he hadn't been able to escape, not with prison walls surrounding him, armed guards watching his every move. His heart thundered, the pounding in his ears a deafening cadence.

"Are you okay?"

The soft voice jolted him. He looked up to see Nina at the table, her worried gaze roaming over his face. Her kindness washed over him like a balm.

He fussed with the flatware, arranging it precisely on the table. "I'm fine."

She hesitated a moment more, her gaze searching, then hurried back into the kitchen. He couldn't resist a quick glance down at her hips, provocative temptation as they swayed side to side. He wrenched his gaze away.

The Sacramento Bee sat in a messy stack on the end of the counter, interspersed with sections of the *Reno Gazette*. He rose and ambled over to the counter and looked through the folded newsprint. He separated the two newspapers into neat piles, ordered by section. Then he picked up the front page of the *Bee* and turned to take it back to his table.

Suddenly, there was Nina, with a steaming plate in her hands. Letting go of the newspaper, he reached out to steady her when she nearly stumbled with surprise. His hands lingered on her shoulders, the contact impossible to sever, inconceivably sweet.

Her face tipped up, she locked her gaze with his, her lips parting. He clearly remembered their taste, the exact degree of warmth when he'd pressed his mouth to hers. The curl of her breath against his cheek, the sound of her sighs as pleasure mounted. His body had stored every touch, every sensation, the images burning under his skin in erotic detail.

He had to pull away. He tried to lift his foot, to take a step back, but he felt as immobile and unyielding as the cold gray stone of Folsom Prison. Yet if he didn't get his hands off her, he'd be pulling her close in another moment, pushing his way into her life just as he had five years ago.

She took the step back, thank God. Took a breath, which lifted her breasts and drew his gaze again. But at least that step took his hands from her shoulders, forced him to drop them back at his sides.

Hands shaking, he bent to pick up the paper he'd dropped. By the time he straightened, she'd set down the plate of meat loaf and mashed potatoes and retreated behind the counter.

Resolutely, he returned to the booth, setting the front page of the *Bee* next to his plate. He risked a glance over at her, but that was enough to chase Nina back into the kitchen. He could see her framed by the pass-through window, her dark brown eyes huge in her face.

"Let me know if you need anything else," she called out from the kitchen.

There was something he needed, with a heat so intense it would incinerate them both. But that wasn't what she meant.

So instead, he tried to think of something he could ask her for, a way to bring her back out of the kitchen. There was ketchup on the table and plenty of gravy on the potatoes. The vegetable was peas; not one of his favorites, but he'd learned to eat everything offered to him at Folsom. He would like some bread to sop up the gravy, but out of reflex, he squelched the request.

"I forgot your roll," she said, startling Jameson, making him wonder if she'd read his mind. As he'd hoped, she left the kitchen, pulled out the steamer drawer behind the counter and dropped a roll on a bread plate.

She brought it to him, setting it on the table. Her gaze was wary.

He breathed in the yeasty fragrance of the whole wheat roll. "Does your mother still do the baking?"

"I do," Nina said, then she added grudgingly, "I own the place now."

"Your folks—"

"They're retired." She gestured to his plate. "Eat. Before it gets cold."

She backed away, looking a bit edgy now. She glanced back over her shoulder at the clock above the kitchen, then at him, then at the door to the café. His instincts made preternaturally sharp by four years of confinement, unease roiled within Jameson.

He pushed aside his discomfort and took a bite of meat loaf, then the potatoes and gravy. He thought he'd never tasted anything so delicious. He sighed and leaned back with his eyes shut for a moment, savoring the flavor.

"I have work to do," she said again, but she didn't step away from his table.

"Go ahead," he told her. "I'm fine."

Behind him, he heard the bell jangle as the door opened. Nina's edginess gave way to fear as she glanced from the door to his face. What the hell?

"Mommy!" The childish shout cut through the quiet of the empty café.

Now Nina moved away from Jameson, quickly intercepting a young boy wending his way through the tables toward her. She picked up the boy and held him close, then hurried past Jameson toward the kitchen.

It didn't take a genius to figure out why Nina was so determined to keep her son away from Jameson. What mother in her right mind would want her child exposed to a loser ex-con like him?

Chapter Two

Her heart hammering in her ears, Nina stood in the kitchen just out of sight of Jameson, clutching her son Nate close to her chest. She trembled all over, her knees so weak she had to lean against the prep counter. Her arms tightened reflexively, the drive to keep her son safe pounding through her.

Angling herself a bit, she peeked through the kitchen pass-through. As if he sensed her focus on him, Jameson lifted his gaze to hers. Trapped by his scrutiny, she couldn't move.

Had his eyes always been so impossibly blue? Had his arms always rippled with taut muscle or had prison laid down those striations of tension? It had only been one night, yet she could still remember the feel of his hair-roughened flesh against her palms.

"Mommy, let go," Nate said, his mouth mashed against her collarbone. "I want down."

Finally she tore her gaze from Jameson's and stepped out of view. As she dragged in a shaky breath, she had to quell the urge to run, to make a dash for the café's rear door. She could carry Nate up the back stairs to their apartment above the café, keeping him out of sight until Jameson left.

Nate wriggled in her arms and Nina realized the futility of that escape. This four-year-old bundle of energy wouldn't stand for that much motherly protection. With a sigh, she loosened her arms and let her son slip from them.

"Stay back here," she told him. "Go find your crayons and paper."

He tipped his sweet face up to her, his brown eyes earnest. "I made a picture for you at day care. Got it in my backpack." He twisted to free his arms from the pint-sized red and purple backpack.

"Take it back to your cubby. I'll come look at it when I bring your snack."

He gave her a winning smile. "Can I have chocka chip cookies?"

"And milk. I'll bring them in a minute."

He dashed off to the back of the kitchen where her parents had carved out a place for him when he was an infant. In an alcove that had once been a well-stocked pantry, they'd set up a portable crib, windup mobile and baby monitor. Those essentials had given way to a playpen and toy shelf during the toddler years. Now Nate's place boasted a child-sized table, shelves full of toys and a bookcase overflowing with books. A TV-DVD combo provided emergency entertainment on nights when the café was unexpectedly busy.

Once Nate finished his snack and his interest in coloring waned, he would appear in the kitchen, ready to be her helper. On most Thursday nights, business was slow enough that Nina could keep an eye on Nate as he busied himself with the small tasks she gave him. Tonight, she'd just have to make sure she kept her son occupied in the back until Jameson was safely gone.

The door bells jangled and Nina looked up, hoping the night cook had arrived for his shift. She welcomed any distraction to defuse the tension that crackled through her. But it wasn't Dale, just an out-of-towner couple with two young children. No doubt they were on their way to Tahoe or Reno, making an early weekend of it.

As she stepped from the kitchen to bring them menus, another family entered, this one with grandma and four children in tow. Nina grabbed seven more menus as the two groups joined forces and started rearranging tables in the middle of the café. She waited at Jameson's table as parents helped their children with their jackets before seating themselves.

Jameson wiped up the last of his gravy with his roll. "Early dinner crowd. Especially for a Thursday."

She didn't want to respond, didn't even want to acknowledge that he was there. Why wouldn't he leave? "It's a church group from Sacramento. They've been in before."

A third family jangled through the door, this one led by the church pastor. Their arrival brought the count up to nearly twenty. Nina added several children's menus to her stack and left them on the row of tables the group had put together.

In the kitchen, Nina ran through the possibilities in her mind. She could call Lacey back. She could phone her mother, but Pauline Russo needed to be home with her husband, not cooking at the café. Nina's father was still recovering from a mild heart attack.

Or, she could ask…no, she wouldn't even consider it. She wanted him gone, the sooner the better. She shut her eyes, trying to think.

"Where's the night cook?"

She jumped at the sound of his voice and took a quick step back. She hadn't even heard his quiet footsteps into the kitchen. "He's a little late."

Jameson nodded, his intense blue gaze never leaving her face. "You can't wait tables and put up orders by yourself."

She wrapped her arms around her middle. "He'll be here soon."

Jameson nodded. "You'll give my number to your folks?"

"Yes, I will." *Now go. Please.*

He nodded again, then turned away. He'd nearly stepped from the kitchen when the café phone rang. Back in his alcove, Nate called out, "I'll get it, Mommy!"

Jameson stopped, looking back over his shoulder as Nate raced for the old-fashioned dial phone on the kitchen wall. As Nate snatched up the receiver, Jameson turned to watch the tiny whirlwind.

"Nina's Café," Nate said importantly. "May I help you?" He listened a few moments, then held out the phone to Nina. "It's Dale. He's sick."

Nina sent up a silent prayer that Dale was faking and could be bullied into coming into work. But she only had to hear the few raspy words the young man could muster to realize he was genuinely ill, victim to the latest strain of flu.

"Take care of yourself, Dale." Nina hung up the phone, then looked out at the tables of hungry customers.

"Nina," Jameson said.

She didn't even think before she answered. "No."

"Let me help you."

She shook her head. She couldn't think when he was here. If he would only leave she could come up with a solution to her dilemma.

Nate tugged her hand. "I can help, Mommy. I can fill all the sugar shakers and all the salt and peppers."

"Lacey filled them already, sweetheart." Nina put her arm around her son and led him back to his alcove. "I'll bring you your cookies right now."

She hurried to the dry store shelves and pulled out the plastic container of homemade cookies. She grabbed a handful and put them on a paper plate, then stopped in the walk-in refrigerator for a carton of milk. She brought cookies and milk to Nate, then found his cartoon cup.

"I'm going to call Grandma," she told him. "She'll take you to her house tonight."

She couldn't impose on her mother to come in to work, but Pauline would never pass up a chance for a visit from her grandson. Leaving Nate munching cookies and drawing on an art pad, Nina returned to the kitchen.

A glance out at the floor told her the crowd had grown, three new parties staking out their own territory in the café. As she watched the latest arrivals settle in, she remembered the item in the *Sacramento Bee* about a church convention in Reno this weekend. It seemed every congregation in the Central Valley had made the detour to her café on their way up Interstate 80.

When she didn't see Jameson, she felt grateful and anxious all at once. So he'd left. That was just what she wanted, right? It was crazy to feel so abandoned.

Grabbing the phone, she dialed her parents' house. She focused on her father when he answered, heard the tiredness in his usually hearty voice.

"It's bingo night, honey," Vincent Russo reminded her. "Mom won't be home until ten."

Nina rubbed at the tightness between her eyes. Thursday had been bingo night for her mother for at least a decade. Jameson's presence had so scrambled her brain, she'd clean forgotten.

"She's got her cell, hon," her father said. "You can call her there."

"That's okay, Daddy. I'll call her later." The last thing she wanted was to deprive her mother of that small weekly pleasure.

Hanging up, she returned to Nate's cubby. "Grandma's busy tonight. You'll have to stay here, sweetie." She turned on the TV-DVD combo.

"Yay! A video!" Nate went down on hands and knees to search the DVDs on the bottom bookshelf. He pulled one out. "This one."

Nina set up the Disney movie and gave Nate the remote. "Finish your snack first. Then you can start the movie." She hurried back out to the kitchen.

She nearly stumbled when she saw Jameson at the prep counter, a white apron tied around his waist, his deft hands slicing tomatoes. "I think they're ready to order."

"What are you doing? You can't be here."

He speared her with his gaze. "You've got nearly thirty customers out there and you don't have a cook."

She looked out on the floor and saw three more families had arrived. "I'll find someone else."

"You don't need to. I'm here."

Panic flared inside her. The longer he stayed, the greater the risk that he might guess. She couldn't let that happen. She had to protect Nate. "You need to leave." She bit out the words, her fear making her harsh.

"I know you don't want me around your boy." His shoulders tensed, his hands stilled. "I'm the world's lousiest role model, I know that. If he was my son…"

He's not! He's not your son! She wanted to shout the words.

"I just want to help." He looked back at her. "I won't talk to him, okay? I'll keep my distance."

A heaviness settled in Nina's stomach. It felt wrong to let him believe she wanted him to go because he was an ex-con. Yet how could she tell him the truth when it left her so vulnerable?

The noise level out on the floor increased as another party entered. Jameson stared at her, waiting for her answer. She nodded. "I'd appreciate your help."

She saw a flicker of gratitude in his eyes before he turned away and sliced the last of the tomato on the prep counter. "Anything new on the menu I should know about?"

"Blackened catfish. The spice is there." She reached past him for a small shaker.

He should have stepped back out of her way, he knew that. But somehow, the temptation of being near her rooted him to the spot. When her shoulder brushed against his chest it took everything in him to keep from reaching for her.

The contact was obviously unwelcome. She jumped back, the plastic shaker slipping from her fingers into the aluminum square full of tomatoes. When she would have grabbed for it, he plucked it from the juicy red slices and set it aside.

He wiped the blade of the serrated knife on a paper towel and placed it out of the way. "Just the catfish, then?"

"Yes. That's it."

Her hands fluttered like birds as if she didn't know what to do with them. He could come up with at least a dozen suggestions, most of them involving naked skin and hot passion.

She must have seen something in his face because she backed away from him and escaped the kitchen. He watched her through the pass-through as she snatched up an order pad and headed for the largest table of customers.

Jameson tore his gaze from her and focused on the prep counter. He quickly surveyed the familiar layout of makings for cold sandwiches, gravies and sauces for hot food, the griddle and grill behind him. He'd only worked here a year, yet that time stood out with greater clarity than any other in his life. Because of Nina, surely, and their incandescent night together. But also because of her parents, their kindness and trust in him.

Nina put up the first orders on five separate tickets, only pausing long enough to give him the briefest glance before she hurried back out to the next table. He didn't have time to think then, unless it had to do with grilling a hamburger patty or dropping a basket of fries into the deep fryer. They were slammed hard with a steady stream of customers, and he was glad to have his hands and feet constantly busy.

But then the old rhythm settled in and it might have been five years ago, when he had worked the dinner hour nearly every night. His actions became automatic—a quick glance at the ticket, turn and toss a T-bone on the grill, pull the catfish from the broiler, slice open a foil-wrapped baker and toss it on the plate.

If he hadn't let his mind drift a bit from the actions of his hands, he might have missed the flash of movement caught out of the corner of his eye. As it was, he was so occupied with moving the T-bone from the hottest part of the flame, he couldn't turn to confirm what he thought he'd seen. There was a shuffle of feet next, then when Jameson glanced over toward the source of the noise, he saw a small form duck out of sight.

After four years constantly on edge, aware of the peril around every corner, it was a relief to have nothing more to fear than the spying eyes of a young boy. When Jameson heard another rattle, then a clang when a large metal spoon slipped from a counter to the floor, he sensed the child didn't want to be seen so he kept his attention on his work.

He'd gotten only the briefest glimpse of the youngster before Nina had swept him away. He had Nina's coloring—dark hair, lively dark eyes, a sweet smile. Thin as a whippet, unlike his mother's generous body. Energy to spare, Jameson guessed from the way the boy had rocketed into the café.

So, who was the father? Jameson remembered Nina had had quite a thing for one of the local ranchers. That was part of the reason she'd been so vulnerable to him, he recalled with a twinge of guilt. Despite the passion blazing through him, he'd made certain that night she was willing, but even then, he'd known he wouldn't have had a chance if her heart wasn't aching for another man.

So, could the rancher be the father? Had he and Nina linked up after Jameson had disappeared from her life? If so, the rancher certainly wasn't in the picture now, or he would have been the first one she called to stand in for the missing night cook.

Suddenly, there was Nina on the other side of the pass-through, her wary gaze on him. Jameson flushed, half wondering if she'd somehow guessed his thoughts. But she was only there to slap another order on the shelf.

Jameson reached for it, then when Nina made to pick up the slip of paper again, his fingers tangled with hers. She stared at him, startled, her hand tense against his. He had to pull away, shouldn't be touching her, but she was too warm, too real. He couldn't seem to break the contact.

She snatched back the meal check. "Sorry. Forgot to add fries."

"No problem." He turned away on the pretext of checking the steak on the grill. He flipped the T-bone, giving her time to drop the check and go. But when he returned to the prep counter, she still stood at the window, her brown eyes troubled.

"We always worked well together," she said. Then she tipped her head down, set down the check and hurried out to the tables.

Emotion tugged at him, a shadow of what he'd felt years ago when the Russos had taken him into their lives. At the time, he would have jumped over the moon if it would have won their acceptance. And yet he'd betrayed them—once with their only daughter, a second time when he took the path that led to Folsom Prison.

He set his mind back to his work. Take the T-bone off the grill. Serve up mashed potatoes and gravy. Spoon up a dish of peas and put the order up.

He quickly finished the other plates for the ticket, rang the bell and stabbed the check onto the spindle with the other completed orders. When Nina arrived to take the plates out, he made sure he was on his way to the walk-in for more steaks.

As he passed what had once been the dry store pantry, he was surprised to see the space had been converted into a kind of playroom. His small spy had returned to home territory and was now bent over crayons and paper, toys scattered at his feet, a video playing on the TV. The name "Nathan" was stenciled on the wall. Jameson kept moving, his promise urging him on.

They'd reorganized the walk-in refrigerator, but it didn't take long to orient himself and locate the steaks. He tugged a ten-pound box from the metal shelf and pushed open the walk-in door. As he rounded the heavy door, he nearly collided with a three-foot-tall dynamo in blue jeans and Harry Potter sweatshirt.

The boy jumped back, craning his neck to look up at Jameson. "Who are you?"

Something about the boy teased at Jameson, the stubborn line of his jaw, the pugnacious turned up nose. When he recognized the familiarity, pain stabbed at him. That childish face reminded him of his brother Sean when he was ten years old. Because his grandfather had forbidden any visits, it had been by sheer happenstance Jameson had seen Sean that day in San Francisco. Several years older than Nina's son was now, he'd nevertheless had that same innocence in his face. It wasn't until later the rebelliousness and anger engulfed him.

He forced a smile. "I'm Jameson."

The coffee brown eyes narrowed on him. "Are you the new cook?"

"I'm just helping your mom tonight. Are you Nathan?" Jameson asked, remembering the name on the wall.

"Nate," the boy corrected him. "Mommy needs lots of help. 'Cause some of the cooks really stink." ·

Jameson stifled a laugh. "I'm sure they do their best."

"Nope. They're all flakes. That's what Mommy says."

The box of steaks was cold and clammy in his hands, and no doubt he had another order waiting, but he couldn't resist the restless, wiry charm of Nina's dark-haired son. He found himself trying to think of something to keep the conversation going. "I like your playroom."

"Come look," he said, snagging Jameson's wrist. "Papa and Granny made it for me."

Nate towed Jameson along toward the playroom. They'd nearly stepped inside when Nina appeared and blocked Jameson's way.

Alarm burst inside Nina when she saw Nate's small hand on Jameson's arm. She couldn't keep the anger from her voice. "What are you doing with him?"

Jameson backed away. "I'm sorry. I came back for steaks. He was just—"

"I like this one, Mommy." Nate eyed Jameson from head to toe. "He doesn't stink at all."

She took a breath, tried to calm herself. "Go back to your cubby, Nate."

Nate's lower lip came out as he considered rebellion. Then he turned toward the alcove, feet dragging. Just before he slipped inside he looked back at Jameson. "Can you come say goodbye to me? Before you go?"

Jameson glanced over at her. How could she say no? She nodded.

"Sure," Jameson said. "Before I go."

Arms crossed, she returned to the kitchen, Jameson behind her. He dropped the box of steaks on the prep counter and ripped open the flaps. "I didn't go looking for him."

"I know." Nina stepped back out of his way as he crossed the kitchen to the stainless steel refrigerator.

He yanked open one of the double doors and pulled out a plastic bin. "I would never hurt him, for God's sake." He grabbed steaks from the box and slapped them into the plastic bin. Pitching his voice lower he said, "I'm not a damn pervert."

Guilt warred with her protective instincts. "I didn't think you were."

The bin refilled, he returned it to the refrigerator, then glanced out at the floor. "Any more orders?"

"No. I was just coming back to tell you we have a bit of a break."

He pulled down the last ticket, scrutinized it as if it was the Rosetta stone. His dark brown hair, always such a startling contrast to the blue of his eyes, was cut too short to curl the way it had when he'd worn it longer.

She remembered the night they'd been together, that it had started with her brushing a lock of hair back from his forehead.

She never should have touched him. But the loneliness she could usually keep at bay had swamped her that night. She'd seen Tom Jarret in the café, and the hopelessness of her love for him had hit her hard. She'd gone back into the kitchen for a quiet moment to collect herself and there was Jameson, his intense blue eyes reading her soul.

Nina shook off the old memories and hurried out to the register where a customer waited. She rang up the sale, then took out a bus tray to clear the dirty dishes. Once the tables were clean, she took the dishes back to wash. Sending the backlog of four bus trays through the sterilizing dishwasher took nearly twenty minutes. By then, Jameson had dinged the bell for the last order.

As she carried the plates out to the last table of customers, Nina's conscience hounded her. *You ought to tell him,* an inner voice demanded. *He has a right to know.* But if Jameson knew the truth, Nina would no longer be in control. There was no telling what he would do and whether she could keep Nate safe.

Vehicular manslaughter. She didn't know all the details of what had sent Jameson to prison, but she knew that much. He'd driven a car head-on into another and killed the driver and passenger. He'd pled guilty and been convicted.

The Hart Valley busybodies had had a field day when they'd heard. *Jameson O'Connell was always such a wild boy,* they said when word of the twelve-year sentence filtered down. *He was always headed for trouble. He finally got what he deserved.*

Could he be out on parole already? It had been only four years—not nearly a long enough sentence for killing two people.

Nina sorted flatware into a partitioned tray, then carried the tray back out front. When she returned to the kitchen, Jameson was scraping down the griddle with a pumice brick, the muscles of his forearms flexing and bulging as he worked. Nina stared in fascination, remembering how those muscles had felt against her palms as she'd run her hands along them.

When he looked up expectantly, she was tempted to run, and only just managed to stand her ground. "You can take off if you want. I can do the cleanup."

He shook his head, using a scraper to clear the black mess from the griddle. "I like to finish what I start."

Her secret weighed heavy on her conscience as she watched him labor. He'd made some huge mistakes, but wasn't this something a man ought to be told? Did she have the right to keep it from him?

But if she just stayed quiet, let him go on his way, maybe he'd be happier never knowing. "So where are you headed to next?"

She could see the surprise in his face when he looked up at her again. "You mean after I'm done tonight?"

"No, in general. Where are going after you leave Hart Valley?"

He set down the scraper, wiped his hands on his apron. "I'm not leaving Hart Valley. I'm here to stay."

Chapter Three

I'm here to stay.

Where the hell had that come from? Staying had never been part of the plan. There'd never even been a plan, just a vague notion that he'd stop in Hart Valley long enough to speak with the Russos and deal with Sean's ashes. But somehow seeing Nina, working with her again in the café, had changed everything.

But who was he kidding? He couldn't stay in Hart Valley. The town busybodies would chew him up and spit him out, just as they'd done all his misguided life. It would be even worse now, with him fresh from prison, with all the unanswered rumors flying through town like buckeye leaves scattered by a breeze.

Nina stared at him, shocked to the point of horror. "You can't stay."

He sensed something in her voice—simple worry? Or

was that panic? His instincts sent a warning that settled as a knot of tension between his shoulders. "Why not?"

"Because I…because they won't let you. Arlene and Frida and the others."

"The busybodies."

Nina had given the gossiping group that nickname, back when he'd worked at the café. The four old matrons would hold court in the corner booth by the front window, watch him work in the kitchen and whisper about him. When he would emerge to help bus a table or ring up a sale, they would fall into disapproving silence, their angry eyes trained on him every moment.

Jameson grabbed a towel and wiped down the griddle. "Let them talk."

"Jameson, please."

The desperation in her tone sent up warning flares again. "I don't give a damn what the busybodies have to say about me."

"I do." She barely whispered the words.

He felt fingers crawl up his spine. Dropping the towel on the now clean griddle, Jameson rubbed his hands against his apron. "What's going on, Nina?"

She stood frozen, looking trapped. "Nothing." Her gaze flicked away.

His stomach a mass of snakes, Jameson stepped closer to her and grabbed her shoulders. "Tell me."

The moment he felt the warmth of her against his palms he realized he never should have touched her. The thin fabric of her white blouse offered such a frail barrier, they might as well be skin to skin. Whatever self-control he might have once possessed was torn away by the long years of abstinence.

Gripping Nina tighter, he took in a long breath of air, waiting for her to move...praying she'd step away. Because if she didn't, he'd kiss her. And if he kissed her, there was no telling what else he would do.

When she did move it was with excruciating slowness, her hands lifting, no doubt to nudge him away from her. But instead she rested her palms against his chest, and the contact was so unexpected it pulled the air from his lungs, released in a low fragment of a moan. Then her hands drifted higher, and Nina's face lit with wonder.

She was perfect—skin the color of cream, brown eyes endlessly deep, full lips begging his to brush against them. Her mouth curving in a smile, one lock of ebony hair falling across her brow—everything about her invited him in. Her spirit flowed through him like a balm soothing the sharp edges of his soul. He shut his eyes, her beauty almost too painful to see.

Her voice sifted into his ears. "I'd forgotten how amazing it feels to touch you."

His heartbeat thundered so violently he thought it might bring down the walls of the café. If he shifted even slightly he would lose the last scrap of will he possessed, and the result would be mortifying. "Nina," he managed, parceling out just enough breath for her name.

He risked a glance down at her, then cursed his mistake. With her face lifted up to him, her lips moist and barely parted, he would die if he didn't taste her just once.

Any thought that he might resist evaporated when she lifted her face to him. His hands left her shoulders and cradled her head as he touched her mouth with his. She arched against him, her full breasts grazing his chest, her fingers brushing against the sensitive nape of his neck.

He plunged his tongue into her mouth, a distant part of his mind knowing he was taking things too fast, too soon. With a step, he positioned Nina up against the prep counter, thrust one leg between hers. He knew she had to feel how hard he was, the length of him pressed against her hip. But she didn't pull away, didn't push him from her.

He ground against her, knowing he shouldn't, helpless to resist. It felt far too good, impossibly pleasurable. But even as his tongue tangled with hers in her mouth, even as he imagined taking her here in the kitchen, a wrongness began to creep in.

He didn't know where he found the strength, but he stopped, edged away from her. He couldn't look at her, partly out of shame, partly out of fear that the sight of her tousled hair and flushed face would drive him to pull her back into his arms.

Half-blind with the need still burning through him, Jameson walked back toward the sink, took a water glass down from the shelf and filled it. He kept his back to her as he drained the glass.

He heard her light footsteps, sensed her moving closer. He felt the heat of her hand before she touched him, and choked out one word. "Don't."

"Jameson."

Even his name on her lips was powerful temptation. "Don't touch me. I can't—" He didn't finish the thought, hoping she'd understand.

A hesitation, then she said, "I'm sorry." She moved away, putting space between them.

Jameson filled the glass again before he turned to her. She wouldn't meet his gaze at first and when she did, he saw a trace of guilt in her expressive brown eyes. "I shouldn't have done that," she said.

"We both—"

"No, it was me. I took advantage."

He laughed out loud at that, some of the tension in his body dissipating. "Believe me, sweetheart, the advantage was mine."

She blushed, the faint pink an appealing lure. Then he saw the tears in her eyes. "I didn't want to tell you."

He set aside the water glass, risking a few steps closer to her. "Tell me what, Nina?"

She searched his face. "I don't want him hurt."

Confused, he shook his head. "Who—"

He heard the shuffle of feet from the cook area and a small querulous voice. "Mommy? Where are you?"

"Right here, sweetie." Nina turned to go to her son, casting one last glance over her shoulder at Jameson. He followed her, an elusive sense of precognition dancing just out of reach.

As Nina knelt beside her son, Jameson hung back. It was only because he'd promised to keep his distance, not because his intuition screamed at him. Still, as he leaned one hip against the prep counter, his flesh tingled with anticipation.

Nate rubbed at his eyes, then his face split in a wide yawn. Jameson felt his heart squeeze. The lines of Nate's face, the slender body, even the way his head tilted to rest on his mother's shoulder—it all spoke to him, tried to communicate a hidden message. Jameson tried to tell himself it was just that Nina's son resembled Sean as a boy. But tapping at the back of his brain, another voice reminded him he'd only seen his brother that one time when Sean was young.

It wasn't his brother Nate took after. And although Nina's stamp was clear on the boy, the father had added something, too. The father…

A roar started up in his ears and his vision seemed to narrow to just those two people across the kitchen from him. Nate's head resting in the crook of Nina's neck, her gaze meeting his own unflinchingly. The challenge in Nina's face giving way to acceptance as her arm curved protectively around her son.

Her nod was nearly imperceptible, but her words might as well have been a cannon shot. "He's yours, Jameson."

He didn't realize he'd moved until he stumbled into the stove and felt the heat of the still warm griddle on his hand. He snatched his hand back, grateful in a distant part of his brain that the griddle had cooled enough he hadn't burned himself. With an effort, he directed his mind back to the realization that now blared at him.

He's yours, Jameson. Nate was his son. He'd fathered a child on that tempestuous night. He'd done so little in his life that was worthwhile, that had value. Yet somehow, without even meaning to, he'd done something right, helped to create something precious.

The roar in his ears grew louder and he couldn't seem to stand still. Without volition, his feet moved, backing him away from Nina and Nate, sending him from the kitchen, through the café and out the door into the brisk autumn night. He kept moving until he'd reached the Camry, then pulled the keys from his pocket and climbed into the car. He started the engine, backed the car into Main Street, then headed off into the darkness.

He didn't know why. He didn't know where. But he had to get away, he had to run, to think, to find a way to get his mind around the enormity of what he'd just discovered. He didn't know what would happen next, he only knew that for the first time in four years he could escape and that was exactly what he intended to do.

Nina knelt beside Nate, stunned. In all her imaginings of the trauma that might ensue if Jameson discovered Nate's existence, she'd never guessed that he would have simply abandoned her, abandoned the son he'd help create.

Sitting back on her heels, she waited until Nate fell asleep slumped against her, until her legs cramped in the awkward position. Jameson couldn't have left them entirely, disappeared without a word, without declaring he would or wouldn't accept the responsibility and the reality of his son. She'd seen him drive up Main Street, but surely he'd cool off and return.

With Nate in her arms, Nina rose awkwardly. She'd have to take him upstairs to his bed, then come back to finish closing up. Nate would be fine for the half hour or so it would take to lock up, tidy the last table and ring out the register. He was a sound sleeper and once he went down, he was out for the night.

The cool autumn air seeped through her lightweight shirt, sending a chill up her spine as she carried Nate up the back stairs. Nate might be small for his age, but he was still an armful. Nina had to catch her breath on the landing outside the door to their tiny apartment before she pushed open the unlocked door.

She didn't bother with the lights as she crossed the living room toward the minuscule space she'd made over into Nate's bedroom. The apartment had been used as storage when her parents first bought the café. Ten years ago it had been converted into an apartment for Nina. She'd lived here ever since.

And Nate had been conceived up here.

Easing him onto his bed, she tugged off Nate's shoes and jeans then pulled the San Francisco Giants comforter out from under him. After pulling up the covers and switching on the night-light by the bed, Nina brushed a quick kiss on Nate's cheek and slipped out of his room.

As she hurried back down the stairs, she tried to keep her mind on closing up the café. But the turmoil of the last several hours intruded, images of Jameson battering at her mind's eye. Every thought of him spiraled back to the most vivid memory—standing in his arms, his mouth hot against hers, the clear evidence of his arousal pressed against her leg.

She fumbled with the back door latch as echoes of sensation rippled through her. Mixed with her own sensual awareness of those moments, shame burned. She'd intentionally touched him, had invited his caresses, his kisses. It was the only thing she could think of to divert him.

She stepped into the quiet of the kitchen, quickly assessing the bus cart with its trays of dirty dishes, the dessert prep counter covered with cake crumbs, the open spice containers that needed to be put away. This at least would keep her busy, maybe keep her mind from straying back to the feel of Jameson's fingers stroking her neck, his tongue sliding against hers.

Knock it off! She grabbed an empty dish rack and began filling it with rinsed plates and glasses. Blanking her mind as she worked, she kept all her focus on loading the dishwasher.

But she couldn't let go of the tantalizing images. They'd insinuated themselves inside her, linking the more distant memories of that night five years ago with today's brief encounter.

She worked faster, scraping off food, squirting the plates with the sprayer at the sink, jamming them into the rack. But thoughts of Jameson still nipped at her heels, chased deep into her mind. He seemed imprinted on her senses.

The crash of a shattering dinner plate shocked her back into awareness. She stared numbly down at the fragments of crockery, then sagged back against the work counter. With all her heart and soul, she wished Jameson O'Connell had never existed.

At the jangle of the front door Nina realized she'd never locked up, or flipped the sign over to Closed. Picking her way through the pieces of the broken dish, she made her way out to the floor so she could inform the would-be customers she was no longer serving dinner.

The sight of Jameson, lingering just inside the door, hit her hard. He'd taken off the apron and had it wadded in his hands. His face looked wild, as if in the hour since he'd left he'd crawled out of his own personal hell.

He edged away from the door and held the apron out to her. "I forgot to take it off."

Nina moved just close enough to take it from him. "No problem. Thanks for bringing it back."

The banality of their conversation seemed ludicrous. They had a mountain of issues to talk about, yet they were chatting about an apron.

Nina set it aside on the nearest table. "Do you want to sit?"

He shook his head. "I can't." His blue gaze burned into hers. "We have to talk."

She knew that, yet her stomach clenched. "Okay."

He looked down at his hands as if surprised they were empty, then lifted his gaze to her again. "Where is he?"

"Upstairs. Asleep."

"How old…" He swallowed, his throat working. "When was he…" A glance away, then back at her. "Are you sure—"

"He's yours, Jameson. I'm positive."

An incautious joy lit his face for an instant before he squelched it again. "Tell me…tell me how…what happened? We used—"

"A condom. I know." It had been the only flash of good sense in the whole encounter. She'd had condoms in her nightstand and they'd stopped their headlong passion long enough to put one on. "They were old. That's my only guess as to why it didn't work."

He nodded, taking it in. "Why didn't you tell me?"

Her hand gripped the edge of the table. "You know the answer to that, Jameson. You were gone. Vanished. By the time word filtered back to us about what had happened, you were convicted of manslaughter."

The pain in his face was nearly unbearable to witness. "If I had known—"

"What could you have done? How would anything have been different?"

Something flickered in his wary blue gaze. "It might not have changed anything. But I might have—" He cut the words off, looking away briefly. "It doesn't matter. What's done is done."

"Water under the bridge," she said, wondering if he would remember.

The taut line of his mouth eased fractionally into a faint smile. "Your mom forgave a lot with those four little words."

"Mom figures everyone deserves a chance."

His smile faded as his expression turned bleak. "And you? How much are you willing to forgive?"

She didn't answer, but Jameson didn't expect she would. The question was unfair, anyway. His transgressions had gone beyond the absolution of the most forgiving of hearts. And beyond those sins, the potential of his father's legacy still lurked.

Rubbing at her arms, her gaze strayed to the lone table still filled with dirty dishes. "I have to finish closing up. I don't like leaving Nate too long by himself."

"Let me help."

She wanted to say no; he could see it in her face. She forced a smile. "Yes, thank you."

"I'll get the dishes."

She nodded, then stepped around the front counter behind the register. Producing a set of keys, she headed for the door and locked it. After flipping the sign in the window, she shut off the front lights. The whole time she kept her back to him, giving him the clear impression she wished him gone.

But they still had plenty to resolve and he wasn't leaving until they'd talked everything out. Guilt dug at him that his first instinct had been to run, but he'd gotten his head on straight quick enough and he was determined to take responsibility. He welcomed it.

He quickly cleared the table, stacked the dishes efficiently and carried them back to the dishwasher. The stack filled the rest of the rack that Nina had started. He shoved the rack into the dishwasher, started the cycle, then dumped the dirty flatware into a rack for the next load.

He heard the beeps of the register as Nina rang out the day's sales. He could see her shoulder and the curve of her hip through the kitchen doorway and he let himself relive the brief unforgettable moment of their kiss. Right then, he would have given another four years of his life to kiss her again.

Once he'd pulled the sterilized rack from the dishwasher and shut the doors on the flatware, he headed back out front. Nina was counting up the register, credit card slips in a neat pile next to currency of varying denomination.

He waited until she'd counted through the tens in her hands and noted the total on the daily receipts sheet, then he stepped into her line of sight. "We're not finished."

She compressed her lips and a dimple formed in the corner of her mouth. He remembered tasting that tiny depression, laving it with his tongue. He shut down his thoughts, focused on Nate, his future.

She sighed. "Yes."

"Who knows I'm his father?"

"No one," she told him flatly.

"You must have told your parents."

She shook her head. "Not even them."

A dull ache centered inside him. "What about Nate?"

She met his gaze. "I told him you lived somewhere else and you couldn't come to visit."

Nothing but the truth. Still, it cut deep. "And now that I'm here? What do we tell him?"

"I don't know. I haven't had thirty seconds to even think about it."

"We don't have to tell him about prison. Not yet."

Her dark brown eyes flashed. "We don't have to tell him anything!"

"Fine. Other than that I'm his father—"

"I'm not telling him that."

He thought he would explode with anger. "The hell you won't!"

"He's only four. He won't understand."

"He'll understand that much." Tamping down his ire, he took a step toward her, risked a hand on her shoulder. "Nina, please…"

He felt resistance, as if she wanted to shrug off his hand. She took a breath, let the contact remain. "What do you want, Jameson? To let the world know you're his father, then head off down the road? You said you want to stay, but how long will that last?"

How could he answer that, when he hadn't even worked it through in his own mind? "He needs to know who his father is."

She nodded, a bare concession. "I think you're right.

But it will break his heart to meet his father, then be abandoned."

"I won't abandon him."

The beginning of tears glimmered in her eyes. "How do I know that, Jameson?"

What could he say to her, what could he promise? His own father was such a sorry excuse for a man. He might not have followed in his father's footsteps, but he had his own trail of failure. How could he prove to Nina he could change, that he could be the kind of dad Nate deserved?

What burst into his brain, half formed and half crazy, he should have rejected out of hand. Even if he had the courage to say it out loud, she'd never agree. It was a fantasy anyway, something that worked for people like the Russos, but for a man like him, happily ever after was a joke. Especially with the possibility he was more like his father than he wanted to believe.

But this wasn't for him. This was for Nate. He'd discovered he had a son and he would damn well do everything he could to build him a better life than he'd had.

He swallowed against a desert-dry throat, taking a deep ragged breath. His gaze locked with Nina's, he tightened his hand on her shoulder.

And forced the words out. "Marry me."

Chapter Four

He saw the rejection in her eyes even as she took a breath to voice it. He put his hand over her mouth to stop her, then had to steel himself against his reaction to her soft lips against his palm. Her gaze widened, an echo of his own physical response in their dark brown depths, and desire curled even tighter within him.

Nina stepped out of reach. "No."

"Nina, please. Just think it over—"

"No! I don't have to think anything over." She shook her head, retreating another step into the kitchen. "You're crazy. Marry you…I don't even know you. I don't want to know you."

Her words cut deep, spawning anger. "I'm the boy's father."

"Nate." She tipped her head back, challenge in her dark eyes. "His name is Nate. And you were a sperm donor, not a father."

"I didn't even know he existed."

"You and I both know I had valid reasons for keeping that to myself."

It shouldn't hurt anymore. His years in prison should have made him numb, should have dulled the sharp edges of his emotions. But the judgment of the court was nothing compared to Nina's scorn.

If only he could rewrite history…

He might have made a different choice that night in Sacramento. Might have taken a different path, might have…abandoned his brother. But could he have chosen his son over Sean? The look of confusion on her face at his brooding silence jarred him from his thoughts.

"I understand you were put in a difficult position," he acknowledged. "I only know that now I want to do the right thing."

She crossed her arms over her middle in a gesture of self-protection. "The right thing would be for you to leave. Get out of our lives."

It should have been easy to walk away. To step back from the responsibility, from a son who didn't know him, who by all rights would probably be better off never knowing him. He made a lousy role model. He'd never made anything of himself. His one supreme sacrifice had been a lost cause that couldn't save anyone— not the people in the other car, not even his brother.

Yet something kept him rooted to the spot. Something within him screamed out his objections. There was a chance here, for redemption, for retribution, for rebirth. Salvation lay in the small, compact body of a sweet-faced four-year-old boy.

His boy.

Jameson dug deep for fortitude. "I need to be part of his life, Nina."

She hugged herself tighter. "No."

"One way or another, Nina. I will be part of his life."

Her brown gaze narrowed. "Meaning what?"

"You can't keep him from me." His stomach churned as he forced out the words. "I have rights."

"No, you don't. I'm his mother. You're nothing to him."

"I want to be something." Desperation to make her understand moved Jameson nearer. He hated himself for the fear he saw in her face, just as he'd hated his father for putting that look in his mother's eyes. But he couldn't back down. He had to find a way to make her agree.

"Nina..." He touched her lightly on the shoulder and she shivered. "It doesn't have to be...a conventional marriage. We don't have to..."

She swallowed and the movement of her throat mesmerized him. He shook his head, trying to clear it. "We can share a house, share a life, but not..."

What would the delicate skin of her throat feel like against his palm? If he grazed his lips along the curve from jaw to collarbone, would her pulse quicken against his mouth? Tangled in his imagination, he lost the thread of their conversation.

"Jameson..." she said, the words barely a whisper.

It wasn't invitation in her voice, but he couldn't resist bending his head down to hers, to taste his name on her lips. It wouldn't do a damn thing to advance the cause of marrying him, but in that moment he couldn't think of a thing except kissing her.

* * *

She couldn't let him kiss her again. As bad a mistake as it had been earlier, now the lunacy of his marriage proposal hung over her. The moment he touched her nothing else mattered but his heat. She had to protect her son, not give in to the longings Jameson set off with just a brush of his fingertips against her skin.

His lips hovered over hers, nearly too close to resist. She mustered her resolve and stepped aside, then skirted him so she could gain some space. She backed into the café's dining area, striking her ankle on a chair leg. She used the pain to bring her back to her senses.

"I want you to leave." The words weren't quite steady, but clear enough. "Please go."

He took a step toward her, but now she had the space to retreat. "Jameson, please."

"I'm not leaving until we settle this."

"We have. I won't marry you."

"Nate needs a father and I'm it. I won't ask you for anything in our marriage except to be his mother. I'll stay out of your bedroom. But you will marry me."

"I won't! You can't force me—"

He closed the distance between them so rapidly, she didn't have a chance to so much as breathe, let alone escape. He wrapped his hand around her wrist, gentle but implacable.

"No, I can't force you." The words were laden with quiet menace. "But I will do everything in my power to assert my parental rights."

"You're an ex-con—no judge in his right mind would grant you visitation, let alone custody."

"My grandmother, on the other hand, is a fine, upstanding citizen, with more money than she could ever spend in a lifetime. She'd be thrilled to know she has a great-grandson. I'm sure she'd be more than happy to act as his guardian."

Horror filled her. "You wouldn't take him away from me."

Something flickered in his face and he glanced away from her. Then his gaze grew as hard and cold as polished lapis. "Marry me, Nina."

A hole opened inside her, threatening to envelop her. She tried to think, but her thoughts kept chasing each other, an endless loop of fear. She'd barely known Jameson five years ago—now he was a complete stranger. But was he capable of the ultimate cruelty? Would he take Nate away from her?

He wouldn't because she wouldn't let him. She would pack up Nate and abandon her home, her business, her family, before she would give up her son.

She needed time, enough space to think things through. "Please, give me a night. Come back tomorrow and we'll—"

"When tomorrow?"

She tugged her captive hand and relief washed over her when he released her. She could still feel the imprint of his skin against hers. "Nate goes to preschool at nine. Give me until ten to set up for lunch. Then we'll talk."

He nodded, but his gaze roved over her face as if searching for duplicity. She blanked her expression, quieted her thoughts, refused to flinch as his visual exploration passed over her like a caress.

"Tomorrow," she said, injecting as much conviction as she could into the word. "I promise."

"I just want to do what's right, Nina."

The fervency in his simple vow clutched at her heart. She hardened herself against the feeling. "Then why won't you just go?" Away from them. Out of their lives.

Jameson's throat worked. "Because he needs me."

"He doesn't even know you."

"But he still needs me."

He pulled away then, giving her a wide berth as he headed for the door. She waited until she was certain he was gone, then hurried over to lock the front dead bolt, giving the handle a tug to be certain the bolt was thrown. She had to resist the irrational urge to further bar the door by pulling a table in front of it.

Keys in hand, she wound her way back through the dining area, her steps moving faster as she moved through the kitchen. Taking the back stairs two at a time, she quickly ran through a mental list of necessities she would have to take with her.

They had to escape. It was the only way to keep Nate safe—from a father he didn't know, from the risk of being stolen from his home, ripped from his mother's arms. Their only option was to flee.

Stepping quietly into Nate's room, she slid the closet door open and retrieved the small suitcase her son used on his overnights with Grandma and Grandpa. She could load it with enough changes of clothing for two or three days, then buy whatever else they needed on the road. His toy chest wouldn't possibly fit in the trunk of her small car so she'd have to pick a few of his favorites to bring. It would be hard to explain why he'd have to leave behind so many beloved treasures, but she had no choice.

She set the suitcase on the floor beside Nate's dresser and pulled open the top drawer. Best to take extra underwear. Nate hadn't had an accident in months, but with the stress of leaving home, he might regress. She grabbed up a handful and was about to drop it in the suitcase when she heard a light rap on the apartment door.

There was no doubt who'd just knocked. There was no denying him entry. He'd probably pound the door even harder, and Nate would wake.

A handful of Nate's Spider-Man underwear gathered close to her chest, Nina went to open the door. Jameson stood on her small landing, head down, shoulders slumped. His head swung up and his gaze took in the small bundle in her arms.

"Please don't leave, Nina."

"I wasn't—" She cut off the transparent lie. "I only want to keep him safe."

"So do I. I swear it to you."

"But if you take him, pull him away from the only home he's known…"

Jameson stared down at her, his silence just as damning as the spoken truth. What could she have been thinking? Tearing Nate from everything familiar to him, the grandparents he loved deeply…whose safety would she preserve by running away?

Tears burned her eyes, tightened her throat. "I don't want to marry you."

"I know I'm not nearly the man you deserve." He held his hands out, palms up as if seeking his future…or coming to terms with his past. "Until now, I've made nothing of myself. Yet somehow I created something good, something right. I can't just walk away from that."

"But why marry me? Can't you be part of his life without that?"

"I want him to see us together. He needs us both." He dropped his hands to his sides. "Give me two years, Nina. Just two. Enough for Nate and me to get to know each other, to build a bond. Then, as long as I'm still in his life…we wouldn't have to stay married."

She wanted to say no. Uniting herself with Jameson terrified her. Her careful control over her life would be shifted if she let another person in.

She had to say no.

He reached for her as if to stop the word he must have sensed. "Please, Nina. Marry me."

Dragging in a breath, she groped for strength. "Yes. I will."

Late afternoon sunshine filtering through the pines striped Main Street with gold and set off an inexplicable ache in Nina's chest. She'd forced herself to sit on the bench in front of the café, unwilling to give in to the nervous energy skittering up and down her body. Jameson leaned against the mailbox out in front of Janine's Style & Cut, his hands jammed in the pockets of his jeans. He stood perfectly still and she might have believed his false air of calm if she didn't see the tight set of his jaw, the convulsive working of his throat.

"Shouldn't he be here by now?" Jameson asked, his tone rough and impatient.

"Ten more minutes," she promised. "The preschool bus drops him off at three-thirty."

He lapsed back into silence, his gaze fixed on the Hart Valley Inn across the street. The innkeeper, Beth

Henley, stepped out with her broom to sweep the walk, and she smiled and waved at Nina. She directed her friendly smile toward Jameson and he gave her a brusque nod in response. Nina could see the questions in Beth's face when the innkeeper turned back to her, but Nina wouldn't be giving anyone any answers until she'd broken the news to the three most important people in her life.

Once she'd acquiesced to Jameson's proposal last night, they sat in her small living room and spoke quietly about what would happen next. They planned to tell Nate first, as soon as he returned from preschool. Nina had already arranged to have dinner at her parents' tonight where she would make her announcement to the rest of her small family.

Jameson shifted, pushing away from the mailbox to pace a few steps along the curb before returning to his post. "You didn't say anything to him this morning?"

"I already told you—"

"I know, I know. We agreed we'd wait until we could tell him together. Sorry. I'm just…"

He paced again from the mailbox to the newspaper racks just beyond the café, then retraced his steps. Nina was grateful Jameson had stayed away for most of the day—he'd had business to attend to in Sacramento. It had given her the space to come to terms with the decision she'd made. If she'd had to cope with his explosive edginess along with her own swings from hysteria to terror to overwhelming self-doubt, she might have run screaming down Main Street.

His brief absence had given her enough time to call Andrea Jarret and ask if she could fill in at the café this afternoon and evening. Nina had hated to impose since Andrea was teaching full-time now at Hart Valley Elementary. But Andrea was delighted to help. In fact, Andrea's stepdaughter Jessie had been bugging Andrea about when they could work at the café again. The ten-year-old had had so much fun a couple months ago relieving Nina when her father had his heart attack, she'd been begging to do it again.

Yanking his hands from his pockets, Jameson turned to face her. "Maybe you were right. You should tell him, without me there. It would be easier—" The torrent of words cut off as he caught sight of the small yellow school bus approaching up Main Street.

Nina rose from the bench and stepped to the curb as the bus pulled up. Used to racing inside the café to look for her, Nate was surprised to see her waiting. He walked slowly toward her, his dark brown gaze shifting to Jameson briefly before he focused again on her.

"Hi, Mommy." He gave her a perfunctory hug, then hung back behind her, his gaze straying again to Jameson. "Hi."

Nina knelt down to eye-level with Nate. "Honey, we're going for a little drive. We have something important to talk about."

He tucked in even closer to her. "Okay."

Jameson reached in his pocket and pulled out a set of keys. "Would you like to sit in the front?"

Nate shook his head solemnly. "Mommy says I'm not s'posed to."

With her son clinging to her hand, they crossed the street to the public lot. Jameson unlocked the Camry and waited until Nina had Nate seat-belted in his booster seat before he climbed inside and started the engine. They pulled out onto Main Street.

Jameson glanced over at her as they reached the end of town. Behind his edginess, hope warred with anxiety. He would never say the words out loud, but she saw his need for reassurance plainly.

Despite her own heart screaming out its reluctance to embark on the course they'd set, Nina couldn't ignore his unspoken plea. She reached across the car and lay her fingers against his arm, giving him a squeeze. In spite of herself, she enjoyed the warmth of his skin just below his T-shirt sleeve. Gratitude flashed across his face and his shoulders relaxed infinitesimally. Nina pulled her hand back, his heat still curled in her palm, and wondered at the small step she'd just taken toward her future.

Jameson sat on the rickety top step leading up to his father's ramshackle cabin with Nina beside him. Nate stood with his back to them beside a fallen log a dozen yards down the weed-choked gravel drive. He had a stick in his hand and every now and then he poked at the rotting tree.

Their announcement couldn't possibly have gone worse. Nate had been horrified, had shouted, "No!" and run away from them. He'd fixed his attention on the fallen log and hadn't looked their way since.

They hadn't even mentioned the impending marriage. Lord only knew what Nate's reaction would be to that. If Jameson wasn't convinced to his very core of the rightness of marrying Nina, of being a father to Nate, he never would have set off this turmoil.

A knot had tightened in his gut. "What's wrong with him? Why is he so angry?"

Nina's worried look intensified the fist of tension inside him. "Give him some time to get used to the idea. We've turned his world upside down."

Over by the log, Nate sneaked a peek at them over his shoulder, but the moment he saw Jameson looking his way, he turned his back again.

"I thought maybe..." He let the words trail off. "Stupid, I guess..."

"What?"

"To think he'd like me. That he'd be thrilled to—" He shook his head.

Nina sighed and a faint trace of her scent drifted toward him. He saw the hesitation in her expressive brown eyes just before she reached over and tentatively took his hand.

He suddenly felt overwhelmed with sensation—her soft breathing in his ear, her fragrance tickling his nose, the curve of her cheek as she leaned close, her palm against his... He needed only her taste to complete the picture.

She spoke quietly, her small hands wrapped around his. "All these years, I've told him you'd gone away."

"It's true. I did go away."

"Yes. And he could accept that because you were never real to him. But now here you are."

"Why isn't he glad I'm here?" His throat hurt as if the words scraped on their way out.

"Because he wonders why you didn't come before. Why you stayed away all this time."

Jameson groaned. "We can't tell him why."

"Not yet. But we'll have to someday, when he's older. It's not something we can keep from him forever."

"You're right." He thrust aside the futile wish that he could wipe away that part of his past. "He'll have to know."

He turned to her and realized she was near enough that he had only to tip his head the slightest bit to press his lips against her brow. Her eyes flickered with heat, then a wariness crept in. She leaped to her feet, breaking the contact between them. She climbed the steps and moved to peer into one of the cabin's front windows.

"It's hard to believe you lived here. It isn't much of a home." She turned to him, her cheeks coloring. "I'm sorry. That was rude."

Jameson stood and crossed the porch. "No need to apologize. It wasn't much of a life."

The look of sympathy she gave him wrenched at his insides. Pushing aside the softness, he leaned against the cabin's weathered gray wood wall. He made sure he kept a healthy amount of space between them. "We haven't talked about where we'll live."

"I hadn't thought that far." She sighed, the sound like a breeze against his skin. "My apartment is too small. I suppose I could sleep with Nate and you could have my room."

"Not necessary. I looked into a rental today. There's a nice house on an acre outside of town. The old Mc-Partland place."

She hooked her dark hair behind her ear, tempting him to trace that same path with his fingers. "I can't afford that kind of rent."

He looked away to break the image forming in his mind. "I'll take care of it."

"No. That's not right. I should pay my own way."

"Nina, we're getting married. I can pay the rent."

She looked ready to argue some more, then she took a different tack. "The preschool bus might not go out that far."

"Then take him with you when you go into town. The bus can pick him up at the café."

"But on the days I open, he'd have to get up two hours early."

"I'll drive him to school those days."

"I don't want you to drive him!" She shut her eyes a moment, drawing in a breath. "Jameson, he doesn't know you. He doesn't know you at all."

What was he thinking? He was crazy to think this would work. He ran his hand over his face as the answers danced away from him. "If we could just give this a chance—"

The shuffle of feet drew his attention. Nate stood at the bottom of the stairs, scowling. "Mom," he said imperiously. "What am I supposed to call him?"

Jameson remembered how scared he'd been his first year at Folsom facing down a drug-crazed, knife-wielding double murderer. That terror paled in comparison to what he felt now descending the steps to sit eye-level with a four-year-old.

"What do you want to call me?"

This near to Nate, Jameson saw the trace of tears behind the bluster. He wanted desperately to give the boy a hug, to find a way to wash away every sorrow.

Nate tipped up his chin in imitation of his mother's defiance. "I'm not calling you Daddy."

An invisible blade stabbed at his chest. "No one said you had to."

A weight seemed to lift from Nate's small shoulders. "I guess I could call you Jameson."

"That would be fine. What should I call you?"

Nate's surprise gave way to an impish smile. "Spidey?"

At Nina's chuckle, Jameson looked back at her. "From Spider-Man," she explained.

Jameson returned his attention to the pugnacious four-year-old. "Is Nate okay?"

"I s'pose."

They shook on it, Jameson's hand dwarfing Nate's. He heard Nina's sigh behind him, and glanced back to see her eyes bright with unshed tears. She moved past him down the stairs, one hand moving up to her face.

"We'd better go. My parents are expecting us," she said as he headed for the car.

Nate's hand still in his, Jameson followed.

Chapter Five

As they wound up the gravel drive to her parents' cozy ranch-style home, Nina struggled to contain the chaos of emotions tumbling inside her. The sight of her son solemnly shaking his father's hand…the joy in Jameson's face when he turned to look back at her. She didn't know what to feel. A part of her ached because this man, who should be a stranger to her son, had made a small inroad into Nate's heart. As infinitesimal as that step had been, Nina couldn't quite suppress a selfish fear that Jameson might become as important to Nate as she was.

The moment Jameson shut off the engine, Nate had his seat belt off and was out of the car. He pelted up the walk and up the stairs of the wide front porch. Nina's mother had the door open before Nate could pound on it.

"Hi, Grandma!"

Jameson had a stranglehold on the steering wheel. "What did you tell them?"

"I asked if Nate and I could come for dinner." Nina reached for her door handle, the metal cool against her damp palm. "I told her I'd be bringing a guest."

Her mother had asked only if her friend was male or female—an innocent enough query. Nina could count on the fingers of one hand the men she'd gone out with in the years since Nate had been born, and she'd brought none of them to meet her parents. Revealing her guest's gender would open a can of worms before she and Jameson had even arrived.

Rising from the car, Nina watched as her mother pushed open the screen and picked up Nate for a hug. Jameson stayed seated, and the afternoon sun on the windshield no doubt hid him from Pauline Russo's view.

Nate wriggled to get down. "Granny, guess what."

Nina shifted into high gear, hurrying up the walk to fend off Nate's premature announcement. But Nate reached into the back pocket of his jeans and produced a well-folded piece of drawing paper. He smoothed out the sheet and handed it to his grandmother.

"It's a picture of you and Papa and me."

Pauline took the drawing and made a show of admiring it, all the while keeping part of her attention on the strange car. She shot a questioning glance at Nina, then looked even more worried at whatever she saw in her daughter's face.

Nina looked back over her shoulder at the Camry, suddenly overwhelmed by a fervent wish that Jameson would simply start up the engine again and drive away. It would be a terrible blow for Nate, but in that moment, she didn't care. She just wanted her life back to how it had been twenty-four hours ago, before Jameson O'Connell's return.

She squelched her cowardice and forced herself to smile in Jameson's direction. Her focus on him instead of her mother waiting expectantly on the porch, she blanked her mind from thinking about what would be coming next.

Just as the car door opened, she heard her father's voice from the house. "Pauline, who's here?" Then Jameson stepped into view and Nina's mother gasped so loudly that Vincent Russo quickly moved to her side. "What is it?" he asked.

Jameson shut the door and joined Nina at the foot of the stairs. "Hello, Mr. Russo."

"What are you doing here?" The threatening tone her father used was completely uncharacteristic. Vincent Russo stepped in front of his wife and grandson protectively and looked as if he were calculating whether he could snatch Nina to safety as well.

"Sir, we have some things to talk over," Jameson said, his expression serious and earnest. "But first I owe you a very belated apology."

If that thawed her father at all, it wasn't evident in the stiff set of Vincent Russo's still-proud shoulders. "Apology for what?" he asked, not giving Jameson any ground.

"I let you down five years ago when I didn't show up for my shift at the café." Tension radiated from Jameson, translating into a heat Nina could feel despite the six or so inches between them. "I disappeared without a word, didn't keep my commitment."

"If it had been up to me, I never would have given you a chance." Her father stood up even straighter. "But Pauline saw something in you I didn't. Pauline, whose heart you broke."

"I can't do anything about the past," Jameson said solemnly. He turned to Nina's mother. "Mrs. Russo, I hope you can forgive me for the pain I've caused."

Although her mother's eyes filled with tears, there was defiance in her expression. She wasn't willing to make anything easy for Jameson.

He took the first step up to the porch. "And I hope you'll both give us your blessing." Jameson's fingers curled into a fist. "Nina and I are getting married."

Jameson didn't know what was more terrifying—the prospect of Mrs. Russo passing out on the porch or Mr. Russo hauling off and punching him. Although Nina's father appeared more frail than the man he remembered from five years ago, his paternal rage would have packed quite a bit of power. As physically painful as it would have been to be flattened by his future father-in-law, emotionally it would have served as proper penance for Jameson's actions.

But Mr. Russo kept his temper and Mrs. Russo stayed on her feet. Nate seemed unfazed by the announcement; maybe to his four-year-old mind it made perfect sense that his mommy and daddy married. The one Jameson worried about most was Nina, who had withdrawn from him the moment he had made his pronouncement.

They gathered in the Russos' living room. Nina sat behind the ancient upright piano, fingers brushing the keys although she never played a note. Mr. and Mrs.

Russo took the sofa, and Nate the floor where some toys were squirreled away under the coffee table. Jameson perched on the edge of a well-worn lounge chair that he remembered from one of his visits to the Russo house years ago.

It wasn't exactly the third degree they launched at him, but Mr. and Mrs. Russo left few secrets unrevealed as they grilled him. Nate's parentage was news to them, but Mrs. Russo at least seemed unsurprised. Jameson gave them as few details as he could about his conviction and his time in prison, even fewer of how he came to be released. Sean might be dead, but Jameson still felt driven to keep his brother's transgressions concealed.

"When?" Mrs. Russo finally asked.

Nina sat rigidly on the piano bench, looking as if she wished she were a thousand miles away. Jameson couldn't quite erase the guilt he felt about the corner he'd backed her into. He reminded himself that this was the right thing to do, and best for Nate. The boy needed the support of two parents, not the half-life he himself had had.

"We haven't really discussed it," Jameson said, looking Nina's way.

She took a deep breath, letting it out with a sigh. "Soon. I was thinking we might go up to Reno next Monday when the café is closed."

"Would you be spending the night afterward?" Mrs. Russo asked.

Nina's eyes widened. "No."

"We could keep Nate for you—"

"No!" Nina's hand slipped onto the piano keys, and the discordance added to the edginess in the room. "Our marriage…it's not going to be…" She shut her eyes, sighed. "We'll just go up for the day."

Dinner was awkward and Jameson couldn't remember a bite of what was probably a delicious meal. He refused the spumoni ice cream Mrs. Russo offered for dessert and was relieved when Nina declined as well. Nate had already wolfed down a cannoli his grandmother had saved for him and was now cranky and ready to go home.

They stood on the porch, the only sound from the early autumn breeze weaving through the pines and cedars. The easy acceptance Jameson recalled from that short golden time spent with the Russos seemed forever lost. The laughter had seemed so easy then, the smiles so generous. So many nights sharing dinner after the café closed, savoring some special dish Pauline had made just for family. The birthday cake Mrs. Russo had surprised him with. Maybe he had fooled himself into thinking that time had ever existed.

Mr. Russo turned to him, arms crossed over his chest. He spoke softly enough that Nate, out gathering the first fallen leaves, couldn't possibly hear. "I want you to know…I don't approve of this."

Nina looked stricken and Jameson felt as low as a snake. He forced himself to maintain eye contact with Nina's father.

"If you do anything to hurt her—" Mr. Russo stepped closer "—if you so much as make her cry, what I'll do to you will make Folsom seem like a cakewalk."

He was bantamweight and inches shorter, but the older man's dignity gave his words power. Jameson nodded his understanding. "I won't hurt her."

Mrs. Russo nudged her husband aside and reached up to give Jameson a tentative hug. In his ear, she whispered, "I may be an old fool, but I still see something in you."

A little shaken by an unexpected champion, Jameson groped for Nina's hand, not even conscious he was seeking the contact. When she linked her fingers with his, he felt suddenly grounded, as if roots had spread from the soles of his feet deep into the earth.

And a tiny spark of hope lit within his heart.

A blown compressor in the café's walk-in refrigerator put off the wedding for a week, then a doctor's appointment Mr. Russo simply couldn't reschedule postponed the ceremony again. The delay allowed Jameson additional opportunities to get the house ready for Nina and Nate, but also gave him far too much time to think about the gravity of his commitment.

As he stood at the front of the tiny Reno wedding chapel, the weight of that commitment set off a rising panic that expanded in his chest until he struggled to breathe. His suit, stiff and new, felt like a straitjacket and the fragrance of the tiny boutonniere on his lapel threatened to make him sneeze.

Nate, full of the fidgets, had wandered off behind the minister and was picking the petals off the white carnations in his own boutonniere. Nate's moods had flitted from sunny to surly to quiet and withdrawn with quicksilver speed these last two weeks. When they'd arrived at the chapel this morning, Nate had objected vehemently to putting on the small replica of Jameson's suit they'd picked out for him. After he'd lost the argument, Nate had done his best to ignore Jameson entirely.

Jameson glanced over at the minister behind her podium. She smiled serenely back at him. He supposed that was meant as a comfort, but the woman gave him the jitters. He'd never met her before this morning, and it seemed wrong to have a total stranger sanctify their rites.

Movement in the back of the chapel caught his eye. Partially hidden by a tall arrangement of artificial flowers, Mr. Russo paced at the door to the small dressing room where Nina was changing. Lifting his gaze to Jameson's, the older man glared a moment before turning away. The vise in Jameson's chest constricted further.

They'd all driven up to Reno together, Nina in the front seat of the Camry, Nate in back and the Russos following in their own car. Jameson had laid their wedding clothes on the back seat and Nate had played with the zippers on the garment bags, opening and shutting them over and over again for the entire trip. Then when they stopped for breakfast in a Reno coffee shop, no one touched their food.

Nina deserved better than this. Better than a garish Reno wedding chapel with artificial floral decorations and white plastic folding chairs. Better than a rent-a-minister who wouldn't know a thing about Nina's warmth, or her loving, giving nature. Better than a rushed marriage with a man she didn't love.

He was filled with a sudden, crazy urge to call the whole thing off, to march over to Nina and her father and tell them he wouldn't put her through this farce of a wedding. He could put his grandmother's trust in Nina's hands, let her manage it for Nate. Surely no father at all would be better than a father like him.

He poised on the balls of his feet, ready to stride toward the back of the chapel. But before he could take a step, Nate turned and looked up at him for the first time since they'd arrived. The boy smiled, the briefest quirk of his mouth, before returning to his solemn regard of Jameson. Then Nate wandered over and took Jameson's hand. His heart flooding with emotion, Jameson realized it would be impossible to walk away from his son.

Jameson held tight to Nate's hand as a crackling, recorded version of the wedding march swelled in volume. Mrs. Russo emerged from the dressing room and hurried to her seat. Moments later, Mr. Russo took his daughter's arm, and Jameson only caught glimpses through the screen of artificial flowers—Nina's ivory-colored hat, lace gloves, pearls around her neck. Then they started up to the front of the chapel.

Jameson's heart thundered in his ears as he drank in the vision that was Nina. Her knee-length ivory lace dress shaped itself faithfully to her curves, nipping in at her small waist and out again at her generous hips. The short sleeves left her arms bare and she held a small bouquet of ivory roses tinged with pink. The neckline dipped just low enough to reveal the faintest shadow of her cleavage. Jameson's mouth went dry as he imagined following that lacy scalloped edge.

When she reached the front of the church, her father released her arm to Jameson with only the slightest hesitation. Nate's attention strayed back to dismembering his boutonniere, which allowed Jameson to enfold Nina's gloved hand in both of his. He could have stood holding her hand like that forever.

The words the minister spoke blurred. He remembered only two moments of the brief ceremony—

Nina's firm, clear "I do" and his own shaky one. Then he was pressing his lips to hers, wanting to let his mouth linger there a shade longer than he did.

When Nina leaned back from their chaste kiss to look up at him, her lips parted and her dark eyes grew even darker. He would have given anything to be able to read her thoughts, to know exactly what emotions swirled through her in that moment. But the content of her mind, the calm quiet centered inside her, was an enigma to him. He wished he could draw on that silent serenity, find comfort in it.

"I'm sorry," he blurted out.

"For what?"

"This…" He gestured with his hand to encompass the room. "You should have had a nicer wedding."

She shook her head. "It doesn't matter."

Why didn't it matter? Because theirs wasn't a real marriage? Because they'd wedded only for their son's sake? Despite the truth of that, it cut him to have it driven home.

"You're right," he said harshly. "It doesn't matter at all."

The hurt that flickered in her face matched his own, but he didn't feel any satisfaction that she shared his pain. Rather, he felt even worse that he'd inflicted it.

He dropped his hands from hers. "We should go. They have another wedding scheduled." Then he turned away so he wouldn't have to see her face.

Nina glanced into the back seat as they crossed the state line back into California. The excitement of the day had finally caught up to Nate and he slumped against his seat belt, deep in slumber. She wished she could fall asleep as easily, but between the torrent of emotions assaulting her and her exquisite awareness of the man beside her, she felt as wired as a triple-caf espresso.

He'd taken off his jacket before he'd gotten in the car, then had rolled up the sleeves of his crisp white dress shirt, exposing his forearms. His tie had gone in the back seat with his jacket and he'd unbuttoned the top few buttons of his shirt. The enticing vee of bare chest with a scattering of dark hair drew her gaze as effectively as a magnet to steel. It was only with tremendous effort Nina was able to keep her attention from that tantalizing triangle.

She sighed, shutting her eyes and leaning back against the seat. Just when she thought she'd made peace with her decision to marry Jameson, her anxiety and misgivings clamored at her, planting ugly second thoughts in her head. She'd followed through with the wedding despite her inner voice screaming warnings, hoping that once the ceremony finished she would finally silence that cacophony. But if anything, she felt even more torn in a hundred different directions.

One enormous reason blared at Nina, her irresistible, far too intriguing attraction for the man to whom she'd just pledged herself. She'd fooled herself into thinking she could ignore the connections that zinged between them every time they were so much as in the same room. He didn't need to touch her—she felt the contact anyway in her imagination. His kiss after the wedding, as brief as it had been, set off a hundred erotic images in her mind.

It didn't help that her experience with men was so limited. Had she not spent years pining after Tom Jarret, owner of the Double J horse ranch, she might have dated more often, given herself more opportunities for sexual exploration. Instead, she'd pinned all her hopes on a man who'd always made it clear he didn't return her love.

Poor Tom. He'd never been unkind to her despite her constant mooning over him, but he'd never encouraged her either. It wasn't until Andrea Larson arrived in town and so quickly stole his heart that Nina had abandoned the dream that Tom's feelings toward her might change. Married almost a year now, blissfully happy, the Jarrets had become Nina's closest friends.

But in the months since the Jarrets' wedding, she'd turned aside more than one offer to go out on dates. Why? Motherhood certainly gave her an excuse. Sometimes she was so caught up with raising her son, she forgot she was a woman at all and not just Nate's mommy. It was so much easier to push her sexual needs aside.

But now here sat Jameson O'Connell, making it clear that those needs might have been buried, but they certainly weren't dead. In fact, as she opened her eyes to drink in another quick look at him, her desires seemed even sharper.

Somehow she had to keep her crazy thoughts to herself. Resist the urge to run her fingertips over the tendons on the back of his hand, to press her palm against his face to feel the hard angles of his jaw, the softness of his lips. She had to clamp down the unwanted impulse to test the strength of his muscular arms, his thighs…

She wrenched her gaze away from Jameson and out the window to the tall pines and craggy boulders on either side of Interstate 80. Much safer to stare at trees and rocks outside the car than at the man inside it. How she would manage to share a house with him without being driven mad by her own libido she didn't know.

She sighed, impatient and frustrated. It didn't help matters when Jameson reached over and brushed his fingers against her arm. "You don't have to move into the house today."

Glancing over at him, she saw the tightness in his jaw betraying his own anxiety. She turned back to face him. "You know the café's only closed on Monday. If we don't do it today, we'll have to wait another week."

"Your friend Andrea could cover for you. Or your folks—"

"My folks are retired. I don't like asking them to work."

"You're right." He flexed his rigid shoulders. "I was out of line suggesting it."

"No, you weren't." The awkwardness she felt at their situation warred with the empathy for Jameson she never seemed able to extinguish. She gave in to the impulse to comfort him, resting a hand on his shoulder. "We'll move in today. Tom and Andrea have already taken the furniture over in their truck and trailer. Everything else is packed. It's just a matter of loading it into the car."

Truth be told, Nina was afraid that if she didn't take the plunge and move today, she'd lose her nerve by next week. As it was, she still couldn't picture herself in the rambling ranch home where the McPartlands had raised five rowdy boys before they retired to New Mexico. As an only child, Nina had relished invitations to the McPartland birthday parties, fascinated by the noise, the tumult, the clamor of a large family.

She felt like such a fraud taking up residence in a house where that family had been built, where so much love had shimmered in every corner. She loved her son and she could see that Jameson was growing to care for him as well. But with the kind of marriage she and Jameson had agreed to, they wouldn't be filling the five bedrooms of the McPartland house with children.

Jameson slowed as they approached the exit for Hart Valley. Her parents passed them, waving as they continued on to Marbleville where they had a few errands to run. Jameson turned left at the stop and they continued in silence until they pulled up behind the café.

Nate woke and called out a querulous, "Mommy?" Then he fumbled his seat belt off and climbed from the car. He took off like a rocket, racing for the back stairs.

Nate made it to the top of the stairs before she'd managed to extricate herself from her own seat belt and exit the car. She leaned into the back seat to grab her jeans and sweatshirt, her fingers tangling with Jameson's as he reached for his own change of clothes. His hand rested over the back of hers briefly, their gazes locking across the back seat.

He pulled away first. "Sorry." Jeans and T-shirt in hand, he backed out of the car.

Up on the landing, Nate shifted from foot to foot. "The door's locked, Mommy, and I gotta go."

Jameson popped the trunk then followed her up the stairs, so close his heat was palpable. She wanted to slow her steps, lean back up against him to let his warmth soak into her. Instead she took the stairs two at a time to put space between them.

The door unlocked, Nate made a beeline for the bathroom. Nina stepped inside, edging around a stack of moving boxes, clothes clutched to her chest. "You can use Nate's room to change, if you like."

He nodded. "Thanks."

She stepped around him, heading for her bedroom, then shut the door behind her. The room was bare, bed, dresser and nightstand gone, her closet empty except for a handful of wire clothes hangers. The pictures of Nate that had decorated her walls were now carefully wrapped in newspaper and packed in a cardboard box.

Nina dumped her jeans and sweatshirt on the floor and unhooked the back of the dress. She could get the zipper down about to the middle of her back, but no amount of wriggling or contortions would wrangle it any lower. Her hips were too wide to take the dress down and her breasts too generous to pull it over her head unless she got the dress unzipped.

She could call Nate in for help, but recently he'd become more aware of how boys differed from girls. Accidental sightings of his mother in her underwear embarrassed him mightily. Which left Jameson to come to her aid. Her concern wasn't so much that he'd take advantage of the situation, but that she herself would.

It couldn't be helped. Her wedding dress might be pretty and feminine, but it was a shade too snug across the middle. She longed to have it off so she could finally take a comfortable breath.

She opened her bedroom door and poked her head out. She first saw Nate, standing with his hands on his hips. "Mommy! My bed is gone."

"They're over at the new house, sweetie. I told you

that." She craned her neck around. "Do you know where Jameson is?"

Striding from the living room, he loomed large in front of her. "Did you need something?"

He'd already changed and the taut muscles of his chest flexed under the bright lettering, *Nina's Café,* that was inscribed across the T-shirt. Her mother had had the shirts made up a few years ago and had managed to unearth one. She'd jokingly called it her wedding present, although her parents' gift—a dining room set—was already installed at the house.

She never would have thought a T-shirt could be so sexy. Her mouth went dry as her imagination painted a picture of her running her hands across the soft knit, her fingertips tracing the contours of those well-defined muscles. She had to shut her eyes to block out the image.

"Did you need something?" he asked again, now only inches from her.

She opened her eyes and tipped her head up at him. "My zipper," she said, the words barely a whisper. "I can't get it all the way down."

His blue eyes grew darker and his chest heaved as he dragged in a breath. "Turn around," he said huskily.

She did, opening the door only wide enough to give him access to the back of her dress. She braced herself against the feel of his fingertips, then had to swallow hard when they lightly grazed her back. She could tell he was doing his best to keep from touching her, but when the zipper snagged near the bottom, he had to rest the backs of his fingers against her to get leverage.

She felt ready to burst into flames by the time he pulled the tab to the bottom. She quickly turned back around, arms crossed around her to keep the shoulders from slipping. "Thank you," she forced out.

His response scraped out harshly. "You're welcome."

She should have kept her eyes level with his, should never have let her gaze drift down. But some devil in her taunted her, tempted her into seeing if he'd responded to her as powerfully as she had to him. She flicked only the briefest glance at the front placket of his jeans, flushed with the guiltiest of pleasures at the evidence there and thoroughly squelched the urgency to press her hand where her gaze had lingered so briefly. Then she quickly shut the door behind her.

After squirming free of the dress, she sank to the bare hardwood floor and dropped her head in her hands. Oh, heavens, was she ever in trouble.

Chapter Six

As roomy as the Camry's trunk was, they had to tie it down over the towering pile of boxes they'd loaded into it. The remaining load was piled next to Nate on the back seat. There was nothing left at the small apartment but the shabby living room furniture Nina decided wasn't worth moving.

The McPartland house was only a mile out of town, but was well set back from the narrow country road leading there, giving the place a secluded feel. As they cruised up the driveway, Nina couldn't suppress a smile at her first glimpse of the sprawling ranch-style home. As much as she loved the house she'd grown up in, the McPartland place always seemed like a dream house with its wide front porch, expansive green lawn and redwood play set in the back—large enough to keep five rambunctious boys occupied.

Nate's eyes grew enormous and his jaw dropped at

the sight of that massive jungle gym. He was out of the car like a shot, jolting to a stop long enough to ask, "Mommy, can I…?", then was off again when she nodded her permission.

She and Jameson climbed from the car and headed for the back of the house. Nate had scaled the rope ladder and stood poised at the spiral slide, ready to launch himself down it.

A tug of anxiety settled in the pit of Nina's stomach as Nate disappeared into the tube of the plastic slide. "That play structure must be twenty-five years old."

Jameson lightly brushed her shoulder. "I checked it over. No dry rot in the supports and I made sure all the bolts were good and tight."

His thoughtfulness and caring set off a warmth inside Nina. "Heaven only knows how many kids have played on that structure over the years. It's amazing it's survived all that punishment."

He took her hand, held it loosely. "Let me show you something."

He led her around to the other side of the play set where metal poles were set in concrete. Back on top of the structure, Nate shouted down to her, "Mommy, look!" then he slid down on one of the poles. Without missing a beat, he scrambled up a nearby ladder of tires.

Jameson ducked under the structure's cross beam and urged her to follow. He led her to a redwood support for the central platform of the play set. A crude J.O. had been cut into the wood.

She turned to him in surprise. "Your initials?"

"Brandon McPartland and I were friends for part of the third grade. He invited me to his eighth birthday."

His mouth curved at the memory. "Mrs. McPartland was royally ticked at first when she found out I'd carved up the support. But then…" He tugged her a little deeper under the structure. There were all the other McPartlands' initials, even little Michael's, who would only have been two at the time.

Nina's finger drew along the lines of the double M. "I don't remember ever seeing you at one of their parties."

With his fingers still loosely tangled with hers, Jameson stroked the back of her hand with his thumb, a tingling distraction. "That was the only one. Then my mother died."

He said it so matter-of-factly, as if it had been a minor blip in his childhood. She'd been too young to remember when it happened, but as long as she'd known Jameson, she'd been aware of that sadness that had been ingrained in him, soul-deep. He might have used bluster and bravado to mask it, but it had always simmered beneath the surface.

She could see it in his face even now, despite his downcast eyes. She reached up, pressed her palm against his cheek. The faint roughness of his beard rasped against her hand as she caressed him lightly. "I'm so sorry, Jameson."

He lifted his gaze and she saw immediately that she'd stumbled straight into the fire. His hand tightened, locking his fingers in hers. His other hand hooked around the back of her neck and drew her closer to him.

She stood immobile in the brilliance of his gaze. When he tipped his head to slant his mouth over hers, she didn't move, just waited for the first touch. When it was only the lightest grazing of his lips along hers, she was sure she'd melt right on the spot.

A silly notion popped into her head that if they weren't careful, they would set the wooden play structure ablaze with their heat. But that thought brought her back to her senses, gave her enough strength to pull back from Jameson, to break the link of their hands. His gaze was so hot she felt a nearly physical pull back into his arms. She thought she was lost then, that there was no possible way to keep any space between them.

Then he leaned in closer.

The thud of footsteps above them snapped Jameson from the irresistible lure of Nina's soft mouth, her tempting curves. He heard a shuffling, then saw Nate's shadow in the spaces between the two-by-sixes that made up the structure's main platform. "I'm thirsty, Mommy."

To his relief and chagrin, Nina backed away, sidling out of his reach. "Let's go inside, sweetie."

They emerged from the play structure and the late afternoon autumn sunshine poured light into Nina's dark hair, kissing her face. Jameson ached to taste the shadows behind her ears, the creamy length of her throat lit by the sun.

Just as they reached the foot of the slide, Nate burst from the bright orange tube, then ran over to grab Nina's hand. "I wanna see my room, too."

Jameson used the cover of digging in his pocket for the keys to readjust his jeans. "One of these unlocks the back door." He strode across the wide lawn to the back deck. He caught the toe of his running shoes on a warped board and stumbled, then called back a warning. "I haven't finished the repairs on the deck yet. Watch where you step."

He didn't dare look back at Nina, not when he could barely restrain himself from touching her again. Instead he fumbled through the ring of keys, trying to remember which one fit the back door. He had two false starts before locating the right one. Finally, he pushed open the door, then stepped aside to let Nina and Nate enter first.

The back door led into a service porch and laundry room. Nate raced off into the kitchen, but Nina paused when she saw the brand new washer and dryer. Jameson quickly moved up beside her. "I know you probably wanted to pick out your own, but I wanted to have them ready for you. The guy down at Steve's Appliance said these are very durable."

She looked up at him and her smile was like a gentle squeeze on his heart. "They're great. Perfect."

He knew he was probably grinning like an idiot, but he couldn't help himself. "I went with the electric dryer because it was already set up for that, but if you'd prefer propane…"

"Electric is fine."

She continued on into the kitchen. Nate had found the water cooler and the paper cups hung beside it and was guzzling a cup of water. Nina stopped by the butcher-block island and looked around her. Jameson was sure she could see every chip in the tile counters and worn spot in the kitchen cupboards and he kicked himself for not spending more time refurbishing the room. Where he would have found that time, between the carpentry work he'd been doing for a local builder and getting the basics done to make the house livable, he didn't know.

"I'll be stripping all the cabinetry and replacing all

the door fronts," he told her. "I thought a lighter stain would brighten the room. Unless you had something else in mind."

"A lighter finish would be nice. But have you checked with the McPartlands? That seems like a lot of work to do on a rental."

"They know what I'm planning," he said, evading a complete answer. "Nate, ready to see your room?"

The kitchen, dining area and living room were all open to one another. As they cut through the living room, every worn spot in the carpet seemed blatantly obvious despite the recent cleaning he'd given it. Jameson added new carpet to his mental checklist as they turned right down the long hallway. "Yours and Nate's rooms are this way."

He opened the door to the middle of the three bedrooms at this end of the house. "Here's yours, Nate."

As Nate stepped inside, Jameson hung back with Nina. "If he doesn't like it, I can change it."

She was gazing around the room, taking in the built-in student desk and dresser drawers, the rug he'd laid over the worn carpet with a cartoon-style road map imprinted on it. Nate already had the toy chest open and was pulling out the carved wooden cars Jameson had hastily thrown together in the past several days.

Nina turned to him, her dark eyes wide with amazement. "This all looks brand new."

"I had to buy the dresser and toy chest ready-made. The desk I built. If I'd had the time, I would have built it all."

On his hands and knees on the rug, Nate was setting up the cars and trucks on the roadway. Nina picked one up, turned it over in her hands. "You carved this?"

Jameson imagined her seeing every flaw. Spotting a faint scar where the knife had slipped, he took it from her. "Let me take this back out to the workshop and smooth it out."

She snatched it back. "It's fine. It's perfect." She set it back down on the rug and Nate grabbed it, racing it along the imprinted roadway with *vrooming* sounds. "Which room is mine?"

With a hand barely brushing her shoulder, he guided her through the door and down the hall. Just past the bathroom she and Nate would share was Nina's room, farthest from his own at the other end of the house. He'd set her double bed in a cozy alcove at one end and the dresser beside the closet. With all his focus on Nate's furnishings, he'd done nothing for Nina except add a small makeup table.

Nina crossed to the bank of windows lining the far wall and lifted the lid to the makeup table, revealing a mirror on the underside. "Where did you find this?"

"An antique store in Marbleville." When he'd seen the small table he'd imagined her sitting there, brushing her hair, applying lipstick. It wasn't much of a mental leap to picture himself mussing her hair, kissing that lipstick from her lips. With that image burning in his mind, he had to buy the table.

Now as she looked back at him, he wondered if he'd made a monumental mistake. He couldn't quite parse out the expression on her face—worry, unease, a trace of anger.

"You shouldn't have done all this for us."

"I wanted to. I wanted you to feel at home here."

"But you're only renting this place."

"I'm not renting it."

She narrowed her gaze at him. "What?"

Tension gripped the back of his neck as he braced for her reaction. "I bought the house."

Silent seconds ticked by as she stared at him. "The McPartlands have always said they'd never sell. They've been waiting for one of the boys to settle down, move back in."

"They got tired of waiting."

She turned toward the windows, carefully shut the lid on the makeup table. "I promised you two years, Jameson."

"I know."

"If you think by buying the house—"

"I don't." A hollowness opened in the pit of his stomach. "I had the money. The opportunity was there." There was more to it than that, but he didn't want to admit that to himself, let alone to Nina.

"Where did you get that much money?" she asked quietly.

Maybe she'd tried to hide the thread of suspicion in her tone, but he heard it and God, that hurt. "It doesn't matter." Let her think the worst of him; he'd just as soon keep the details of the trust to himself.

She turned to face him. "It does to me."

"The money was mine." He said it as matter-of-factly as he could. "Up-front and legal."

"Okay," she said softly. The light from the window backlit her, giving her the aspect of an angel. The hollowness sharpened into pain.

"This place is too big for just the three of us." He could swear he heard a wistful note to her words.

"Nina…" What could he say to her, how could he explain? When the McPartlands' property manager had told him there might be a chance he could lease-to-own, it had seemed the most logical thing in the world to offer to buy it outright.

But if he dug deep, he knew logic had had little to do with his decision. It had more to do with old longings, and the wishful thinking of a boy whose world was filled with ugliness.

Those longings had no place in his life now. "It was a business deal," he said matter-of-factly. "I plan to rehab the place, put in some sweat equity, then turn around and sell it for a profit. It's a bonus that we'll be able to live here until it's finished."

She looked away, back out the window. "That's a good idea. I hadn't thought of it that way." Then she moved past him quickly. "I'd better check on Nate."

"I'll start bringing in boxes."

She'd disappeared into Nate's room and had the door closed by the time he stepped into the hall. He could hear the soft murmur of her voice as she spoke to Nate, and the boy's high childish voice as he answered. He yearned to go inside, take her hand, press a kiss to her palm, pull Nate into his arms for a hug. He wanted for a moment to feel part of a family instead of the interloper he was.

His hand was on the door, ready to push it open. Instead he pulled away and continued down the hall.

By the time they'd brought all the boxes and clothes inside and parceled them out to the proper rooms, Nina was hot and sweaty and longing for a shower. She'd forgotten to label the box with the towels and it had somehow ended up in Nate's room. By the time she'd located the soap and shampoo, she was moody and hungry and it took all her willpower not to snap at Nate after he'd dumped all his bath toys in the tub.

When she stepped from the bathroom, blissfully clean, a towel wrapped around her head and tucked into a terry-cloth robe, a tantalizing aroma drifted down the hall. Her stomach rumbling, she quickly dressed in jeans and sweater, then followed her nose into the kitchen. She found Nate on a stool at the butcher-block island and Jameson at the stove.

Nate looked up and grinned. "Look, Mommy, I'm making fruit salad." He was picking grapes off their stems and dropping them into a bowl already filled with canned pineapple and sliced peaches.

"Looks yummy." She rounded the island to check what was in the pot Jameson was stirring. He'd showered and changed as well and she didn't know what smelled better—the hearty beef soup or Jameson's spicy aftershave.

"It's nothing much. A few cans of soup I dressed up with this and that." He set the spoon down beside the stove and turned down the burner. When he reached for the cardboard box labeled *kitchen* next to the sink, Nina moved on an intercept path.

Their hands landed on the box flaps at the same time. It took everything in her not to draw her palms up along his arms to his shoulders, the back of his neck, to pull him down to her…

She slid the box out of his reach. "I can set the table."

A tingling sensation rampaging through her body,

she tugged open the cardboard flaps and removed the stack of paper-wrapped bowls on top. The bread plates were just beneath. She unwrapped three of each and carried them to the dining area between the kitchen and living room where Jameson had set up the oak table and chairs from her parents. Setting down the stack of dishes, she turned back to the kitchen.

He was leaning against the counter by the stove, arms crossed, the knit of his T-shirt pulled tight over his chest. One look at the heat in his blue eyes and her breath caught. It took a conscious effort to drag in a lungful of air.

Under his steady gaze, she ordered herself to move. Mechanically, she returned to the kitchen area and fumbled with the cardboard box. "I can't remember what I did with the silverware," she said, emptying the box of its contents.

"It's already put away." With two long steps, he was beside her. He reached around her to open a drawer and his body pressed lightly against her back. "I had to unpack it to get out what I needed to make dinner."

"Thank you." The words seemed to slip out soundlessly on a breath. When he didn't immediately back away, she wondered how she would resist turning toward him.

Then he edged away and returned to the stove. He stirred the soup so vigorously it splashed the wall behind the pot. He set down the spoon and grabbed a paper towel to wipe the spot.

"I'm done, Mommy."

A bit dazed, Nina turned to her son. He held the bowl of fruit out to her, smiling broadly. "Thanks, sweetie." She took the bowl, a handful of spoons, forks and knives, and went to the table.

Jameson brought out the pot of soup, then a basket of rolls as Nina served up fruit salad. He sat opposite her, a relief at first because he was farthest from her, then she realized what a distraction it was to have him in plain view. If he'd sat to her left, in her peripheral vision, she might have been able to ignore him.

He took a roll and tore a piece off. "Do you have to open up tomorrow?" It shouldn't have sounded like an invitation to something extremely intimate, but Jameson's rumbling voice had a way of making the mundane sensual.

She nodded. "I have to be there at five."

"I'll take Nate to school then." He took a bite of the roll and Nina fixed on the way his mouth moved as he chewed. "We're waiting on the plumber at the job site, so I don't have to be there until nine."

On his knees on the chair because they'd forgotten his booster seat at the apartment, Nate spooned up bites of soup and ate fruit salad with his fingers. The electricity between his parents passed unnoticed over his innocent young head. "Can I bring my new cars to show-and-tell? It's my turn."

With relief, she switched her focus from Jameson to her son. "You can take one, sweetie pie."

"I wanna take them all." He set his chin stubbornly.

"There are too many, Nate. It would be too hard to carry them all."

"I can put 'em in my backpack."

"They won't fit," she said firmly. "In any case, you can only take one."

He scowled at her and she saw an echo of Jameson's determination in his face. "I wanna take them all!"

"Nate—" she began.

Jameson's voice boomed across the table. "Your mother said one."

Nate, ready to issue another objection, fell silent, mouth open. He looked from her to Jameson, then back to her and she saw the faintest trace of fear in his face. Anger bubbled up inside her at Jameson's intervention.

Sinking back on his heels, Nate resumed picking fruit from his salad. "Can I take the truck?"

To her shock, he didn't look to her for permission but at Jameson. She saw the query in Jameson's eyes and she gave him a brusque nod. "That's fine," he said.

Nate scrambled from his chair. "Gonna put it in my backpack right now." He raced for his bedroom.

Her stomach in knots, Nina pushed away her soup bowl then rose. She cleared the table of her and Nate's dishes, then turned toward the kitchen. Jameson called out after her. "Nina…"

She scraped the leftovers down the sink, then turned the cold water on high and started the garbage disposal. From the corner of her eye she saw Jameson rise from the table with his own dishes. As she slapped off the disposal and water, Jameson came up behind her.

"I'm sorry," he murmured.

Anger still boiled inside her. "For what?"

"For interfering. It was none of my business."

A sudden urge to weep washed away her ire and she sagged against the sink. "But that's the problem," she forced out. "It *is* your business." She turned to face him and barely pushed out the words. "And I don't want it to be."

The hard lines of his face softened as he gazed down at her. "Tell me what you want me to do."

She shook her head slowly. "I don't know what I want you to do. Part of me wishes you'd just go away or that you'd never…that we'd never…"

He watched her as she tried to swallow back the tears. There were layers behind layers in his face, pain she couldn't fathom, a loneliness so enormous she knew her heart could have never borne it. But empathy was the last thing she wanted to feel for him. That emotion left her far too vulnerable.

She stepped sideways, then returned to the dining area. Setting the empty soup pot, bowl and basket on the counter, she slid them within his reach. She pulled back her hands, carefully avoiding any accidental contact with him, then gathered up the crumpled paper napkins.

By the time she'd disposed of the trash, he'd begun to fill the sink with hot, soapy water. His broad back was an intriguing play of sinew and muscle as he worked.

Her throat aching from suppressed emotion, she stayed in the doorway rather than risk coming nearer. "Do you mind finishing those? I have to run Nate's bath."

He didn't turn. "Go ahead. There isn't much left to do here."

Fortunately, Nate was exhausted by the long day and didn't want to linger in the tub with his toys. He only asked for one story and he was struggling to keep his eyes open before she'd read more than a few pages. When she finished the book and set it aside, she rose to kiss his cheek, assuming he was deep asleep.

"Mommy?" His voice sounded far away, halfway to dreams. "Can Jameson come say good-night?"

She heard the shuffling of feet and realized Jameson stood in the doorway. His reaction to Nate's sweet request was plain on his face—longing, pride, hopefulness. Even as a petty bit of jealousy twinged inside her, she knew there was no way she would deny Jameson this pleasure.

"Sure, sweetie," she told Nate. "He's right here."

She straightened and gestured Jameson toward the bed. After a moment's hesitation, he went down on one knee and leaned close to his son. "Good night, Nate."

Nate woke just enough to reach his thin little arms out to wrap them around Jameson's neck. Jameson hugged him fiercely in return, then let go as Nate slipped back into sleep.

When Jameson faced her, she thought she'd start crying all over again. She'd never seen a man so filled with joy.

Chapter Seven

They fell into a routine the first week—Nina opening the café at 5:00 a.m., Jameson taking Nate over to the preschool at eight before heading off to the work site, then Nina would take a break in the middle of the day and go home. She'd clean up from breakfast, either start dinner in a Crock-Pot or prep something for Jameson to finish before picking up Nate and returning to the café for the evening shift.

Jameson would show up around six o'clock to pick up Nate and take him home for dinner. Nina would help during the dinner rush, then leave the closing up to the cook, Dale. She'd get home by eight or nine o'clock with barely enough energy to eat dinner and shower before falling into bed. Despite her enervation, most nights she slept fitfully, her mind too caught up with thoughts of Jameson. When morning came, she felt like a wreck.

But her grueling schedule had one distinct advantage—she never spent more than a few minutes a day alone with Jameson. He was still asleep when she left in the morning, and she saw him so briefly in the evening she didn't have the time or the brainpower to think about what sharing a home with him was doing to her libido. Her sudden ramp-up in devotion to the café left her too exhausted most of the time to muster even the least sexual fantasy.

Four-thirty in the morning on Sunday, as she sat at the kitchen island hunched over a mug of coffee so strong Jameson could probably strip the varnish off the cupboards with it, Nina pondered her course of action. Tomorrow the café would be dark. Sunday closing time was at eight. That left a stretch of hours and hours without hard work as a defense against Jameson.

She'd expected he would be working at the new housing development in Marbleville tomorrow. But he'd arranged with the site foreman to put in several hours on Saturday so he could take Monday off. He'd wanted a chance to spend some time with her and Nate.

She'd already decided to keep Nate home from preschool, as she often did on her day off. So she would at least have her son as a buffer between her and Jameson. But then the preschool scheduled a field trip to the Sacramento Zoo. By the time Nina volunteered to chaperone, the school had already lined up enough parent drivers. Because they had to limit the numbers attending, Nina would have to stay home. With Jameson.

She stared out the black squares of the windows and imagined the sun sitting sullen and stubborn below the horizon, refusing to rise. She wished she'd done the same, had stayed in bed. In all the years since her parents had turned the café over to her, she had never worked this hard. There had always been the occasional day when the cook wouldn't show or a waitress got sick, but never several endless days in a row when she'd put in more hours working than were humanly possible.

Sliding from the stool, she gulped one last mouthful of coffee before turning toward the sink to dump the last of it. Lack of sleep had taken its inexorable toll and she swayed, momentarily woozy. A sudden thought that she might pass out drifted into her mind as she felt the splash of warm coffee on her fingers. Then a pair of strong hands gripped her waist and she let herself sink back against Jameson's warm bare chest.

He extricated the coffee mug from her hand and asked roughly, "What the hell are you doing?"

She couldn't seem to lift her eyelids. "Going to open the café."

"Not this morning."

In the next moment her world spun as he hooked one arm under her knees and the other around her shoulders and carried her from the kitchen. Her cheek ended up nestled against the hot bare skin of his chest and she could hear the rapid *thud-thud-thud* of his heart.

"I'm too heavy," she murmured, her mouth so close to him, she could have so easily slipped her tongue out to taste him.

"You're not," he said, although the harsh sound of the words seemed to belie the statement.

He nudged open her bedroom door. She opened her eyes long enough to see the rumpled covers. "The bed's not made." She just hadn't had the energy this morning.

"Easier for me to put you back in it."

Why did everything out of his mouth sound like an invitation? Despite her exhaustion, every nerve ending in her body zinged with awareness. As he set her on the bed and tugged the covers out from under her, she realized there was a flip side to her utter tiredness—she had no resistance left to Jameson's compelling sexuality.

Oh, Lord, his fingers were at the button of her slacks. She ordered her hands to move, to push him away, but they remained traitorously at her sides. When she forced her eyes open, she saw the stark need in his face. But his jaw was rigid, as if he were fighting just as hard as she was against temptation.

His gaze locked with hers for a moment and his eyes were nearly black with desire. Then he looked away, quickly pulled down her slacks, took a moment to divest her of her sensible black shoes, then threw the covers up over her.

Sleep lapped at her, like waves too shy to come fully onto shore. She struggled against the pull. "I have to open this morning."

"I'll open. You get some rest."

He stepped back, but perversely, she reached out for him. She caught his hand before he moved out of her grasp. "I should do it. It's my job."

A moment's hesitation, then he dropped to one knee beside the bed. He stroked the hair back from her brow. "Today it's my job. Get some rest, then you and Nate can meet me for lunch."

He rose, but he didn't let go of her hand. She couldn't help herself—she tugged him down to her. She might have wished for some resistance from him to save her from her weak willpower. But he bent over her, yielding to her silent demand.

She wasn't even sure what she wanted—a peck on the cheek, a soft goodbye whispered in her ear—she only knew she couldn't let him leave just yet. He brushed a kiss on her forehead, but that wasn't enough. When he drew back, she raised her head, found his lips unerringly. Wrapping one hand around the back of his neck, she opened her mouth to his.

At first, Jameson held back, the shock of Nina's sensuality shoving the world off its axis momentarily. Then he thrust his tongue into her mouth with a groan and in an instant he was too hard to even think about anything but being between her legs, being inside her. As he covered her body with his, the scrap of sanity still in tenuous control of his brain was thankful they had the shield of the thick comforter.

That frail barrier, and his recognition that he would be taking advantage of Nina's fatigue-wrought vulnerability, gave him the will to pull away from her. His heart thundering in his chest, he gently dislodged her hand from the back of his neck and lowered it to the bed. Remarkably, she was asleep nearly before her hand dropped to the covers. Resisting the urge to press another kiss on her cheek, he backed from the room.

After a quick check on Nate, he hurried to his own room to finish dressing. It had been a long time since he'd opened the café, but as he shaved, he found he could still pull up a mental checklist of the requisite tasks.

He was glad for the chance to ease Nina's workload, if only for the day. He'd intruded into her life, forced her into marriage, uprooted her and Nate. He had to admit that just by being here, he'd made everything harder for her. In recompense, he would ask as little of her as he could, even as his body wanted far more of her than he had any right.

The first morning after the wedding had been the worst. Nate had woken up tired and grumpy, balking at putting on the clothes Jameson had pulled from the dresser, refusing to eat the cereal Jameson had poured, even though it was the kind the boy had requested. He'd wanted badly to call Nina, to beg for help. Just hearing her voice would have been enough, would have eased the panic inside him. But he didn't call.

Keeping up with Nate and his early morning rituals was like following the path of a mouse in a field—every moment he seemed to change direction. Five years at Folsom avoiding gang fights and his cell mate's hair-trigger temper hadn't prepared Jameson for the demands of a four-year-old boy whose life revolved around wearing cartoon character underpants and having peanut butter and jelly sandwiches prepared exactly the same way every day.

But he'd muddled his way through that first day and the ones that followed. By Friday he found he enjoyed sitting across the table from his son at breakfast, eating toast while Nate spooned up sugary cereal. He would search for traces of his own face in Nate's, his own mannerisms in the boy's gestures. He knew he had contributed only physically to this lively, intelligent boy, that he had no other imprint on him. In every other way, he was an outsider.

Dressed and clean-shaven, Jameson grabbed his

leather jacket, then remembered he didn't have the café keys. Back in the kitchen, he found Nina's purse on the butcher-block island and gingerly poked through all the compartments of the cavernous black bag. Feeling awkward for invading her privacy, he came up empty. He realized Nina must have put the keys in her pants pocket.

No big deal. He'd just go back to her room and fish the keys from her pocket. But as he strode down the hall, it took nothing more than the anticipation of seeing Nina warm and slumbering in her bed to provoke his body's response.

He nudged open the door and waited a moment to let his eyes adjust to the blackness of the room. Light from the kitchen barely illuminated this far down the hall, so he'd have to just feel in the dark for Nina's slacks. He wasn't about to turn on the light and risk getting a good look at her.

His foot caught on something on the floor and he bent to grope for it. A faint jingle as he lifted the pants confirmed the location of the keys. As he explored the slacks, searching for the pockets, heat strummed low in his body. God, what a lech he was, when a pair of women's pants turned him on. But this wasn't any woman—this was Nina and every fiber of his being longed to touch her the way he was touching her clothes.

Suddenly, the keys shook loose with a loud jangle. Nina turned in the bed, her soft sigh and the rustle of covers stroking along his nerves. Setting his teeth, he crouched and laid his hand on the collection of cool metal at his feet, picking the keys up carefully to mute any noise. Then he laid the slacks across the foot of the bed and escaped Nina's room.

As he drove into town, he refused to let himself think of Nina, snug and cozy in her bed. He replaced her image with a myriad of distractions—turning on the griddle and setting out the eggs, turning on the dishwasher and making sure every table had setups of napkins and silverware. Focusing on the banal prevented his imagination from leaping into forbidden territory.

A couple of regulars were already waiting out front when he pulled onto Main Street. He glanced at the clock—five-twenty. He had ten minutes to get lights on, the coffee going and the door unlocked. He knew from experience how cranky the locals got when they didn't get their java on time.

After parking behind the café, he let himself in through the rear entrance and flipped on lights as he made his way through the kitchen. Out front, he dumped a measure of grounds into a filter and started the coffeemaker. He powered up the register, turned on the front lights, then without missing a beat, strode to the front door. After reversing the sign to Open, he unlocked the door.

And didn't think of Nina even once. Okay, a lie, but at least he'd kept his thoughts reasonably G-rated.

Two older women in sneakers and sweats entered, followed by two men wearing fishing vests. The men had Thermoses in tow and Jameson hurried back behind the counter to start another pot of coffee. He called back over his shoulder, "Give me a minute and I'll get those filled for you."

"Excuse me, we were first," one of the women declared.

Before he could identify the vaguely familiar voice,

dread dug deep into the pit of Jameson's stomach. He might not readily remember who she was, but his subconscious did. His conscious mind kicked in a moment later, supplying him with a name—Arlene Gibbons. Her companion was Frida Wilkins. Two of the town busybodies.

He took his time getting a new pot of coffee brewing before he turned to face the two women. Arlene peered up at him, her animosity clear in her narrowed gaze. "Where's Nina?" she snapped.

"Taking the day off. Can I get you some coffee?"

"What are you doing here?" Arlene said with venom.

"Running the café," he said, ignoring his knee-jerk reaction to Arlene's disapproval. "Can I get you some coffee?"

"You don't belong here." Her mouth pursed so tight he was surprised she could squeeze words out. "You have no right to push yourself into Nina and Nate's lives."

Arlene had only spelled out the truth—that he was an interloper, a fraud pretending to be a father to a boy he didn't even know. That didn't change the fact that he intended to try, even if he was doing nothing more than going through the motions.

"Have a seat," he said, his jaw aching. "I'll bring you a menu."

He turned to the two fishermen who had sat at the counter. Ignoring Arlene and Frida as he took the men's orders, he slapped the ticket up on the pass-through before grabbing two menus. The busybodies had taken their usual spot near the front window, which forced him to traverse the length of the café with each trip to their table. Leave it to Arlene to make things as inconvenient as possible.

He was back in the kitchen scrambling eggs for the two fishermen when the phone rang. It was barely past six o'clock and alarm burst inside him that some catastrophe had struck at home. He barked out a greeting with far less courtesy than he should have. "Nina's Café."

A moment of silence, then Nina's sleepy voice stroked his ear. "I guess I didn't dream it then. You opened up for me."

He set aside the stainless steel bowl of beaten eggs. "Is everything okay?"

"Fine," she said softly. "I woke up and felt a bit frantic. Just wanted to call and make sure you didn't need anything."

He needed her, desperately, but there was no way he'd lay that on her. "Thanks, but no."

She sighed and he imagined her shifting in the bed, snuggling under the covers. What he wouldn't give to be beside her right now, pressing her close.

"Are Arlene and Frida there?" she asked.

He glanced through the pass-through and saw the old biddy scowling at him. "Yeah."

"Just like clockwork." Nina yawned. "Sorry. Every Sunday, right before their morning walk. They'll be in after church, too, for lunch with the rest of the gang." Another yawn. "You'll have Lacey in by then, but Nate and I can come in to give you a hand."

He should have told her no, that he could deal with the busybodies on his own. But he allowed himself a moment of selfish weakness. "I'd appreciate the help. You get some more sleep now."

"Sure." A long silence. "Jameson…did I kiss you this morning?"

He shut his eyes at the memory and sank back against the wall. He wished he were holding her instead of the cold plastic phone. "Yeah. You did."

"That wasn't a dream, either, then." He listened to her soft breathing before she murmured, "Bye." She hung up the phone.

Blocking Nina's image from his mind, Jameson set down the receiver, then picked up the bowl of eggs again. The hash browns were on the edge of burning, but he managed to turn them in time. It didn't take him long to get the rest of the fishermen's breakfasts together.

By the time he came out to deliver their orders, Arlene and Frida were gone.

The lunch rush over, Nina peeked through the kitchen pass-through at the nearly empty café. Nate sat facing her in the first booth, Jameson across from him. Her son was carefully doling out sugar packets into the plastic caddies he'd collected from all the tables. Jameson was poring over a produce order sheet, updating it with the items they'd run short on during lunch.

Jameson's hair had begun to grow out in the few weeks since he'd arrived and she remembered how it felt this morning when she'd kissed him. Soft, silky. It had tickled her palm, adding yet another sensation to the chaos rocketing through her.

Nate said something to Jameson, then they both rose. Jameson carried the tray full of filled sugar caddies and Nate distributed them onto the tables. In jeans and a T-shirt, Jameson moved with an economy of motion, his forearms flexing slightly from the modest weight of the tray and his back muscles shifting as he turned from table to table. Once he turned to her, a smile still on his face from something Nate had said. Her heart stuttered in her chest at the light in his blue eyes before he returned his attention to her son.

Their son. Parenting Nate was no longer her exclusive territory. As much as she hated to relinquish even a piece of those rights, Jameson was here. And in these few short weeks, he hadn't just been a presence, a figurehead father. He'd woven himself into Nate's world, begun to learn the language of a four-year-old, as if getting to know his son was the most important lesson of his life.

A pang of envy twinged inside her. Years of heartache and struggle and tears had been her hard-won payment for the loving relationship she had with her son. In a matter of days and seemingly with little effort, Jameson had achieved an extraordinary closeness to Nate.

She sighed as she unknotted her apron ties and stuffed the soiled cloth into the laundry bag. Jameson had so quickly taken possession of Nate's heart simply because he was the only one who could have filled that empty space, a boy's yearning for a father. Nate had never articulated his longing—at four he wouldn't have understood it. But Nina knew that piece was missing, had expected it would never be replaced unless she could find a man who would mesh both with her life and Nate's.

To let Jameson in, she'd had to let go of Nate just a little bit. And even as her heart rejoiced at her son's bonding with his newfound father, she couldn't help but grieve for the fragment of his life she'd had to surrender.

The sound of the rear door slamming alerted her to Lacey's return. The young waitress had taken advantage of the lull after lunch to run a couple errands and now would be staying through the dinner hour. Lacey and the cook, Dale, would be handling the café this evening. Dale had called to let Nina know he was on his way and once he arrived, she, Nate and Jameson were free to go.

No more working herself to death to avoid Jameson. She was determined to face up to her unwanted attraction, write it off to old memories and longtime abstinence and simply ignore her importunate desires. She was an adult; surely she could behave in a civilized fashion.

Then Jameson glanced back into the kitchen at her, another lazy smile on his face, and Nina's knees turned to jelly. Heat pooled low in her body and she had to gasp in a breath as she gripped the prep counter. By the time Jameson diverted his attention to Nate, Nina felt ready to swoon.

"Are you feeling okay?" Lacey's query startled Nina and she staggered a step back. The young woman moved closer to press her wrist to Nina's forehead. "You feel a little feverish."

She felt a little hot, but the only ailment she suffered from was suppressed desire. "Get everything taken care of?" Nina asked, breathless. "I could stay a little longer if you—"

"Get out of here," Lacey ordered. "You and your new hubby need a little time to connect."

The kind of connection her body clamored for with

Jameson wasn't suited for discussion in mixed company. "I could wait until Dale—"

"He's here." Lacey pointed out front just as the bell signaled Dale's arrival. The cook lived only a half-mile from town and didn't own a car. "Now get."

Jameson was just putting away the tray and with a nod of greeting toward Dale, he joined her in the kitchen. "Ready?"

Far too much. "Just let me grab my purse." She ducked into Nate's cubby for her bag, then joined Jameson and Nate behind the café.

"Still up for a walk?" His gaze skimmed over her from head to toe. "You've been on your feet for hours."

"You've been working longer than me." She pulled open the back door of the Camry and dropped in her purse. Nate scrambled onto the seat beside it. "If you'd rather just go home…"

Nate piped up. "I wanna see the beaver dam, Mommy."

Shutting Nate's door, she sank into the front passenger seat, grateful to be off her feet. Beside her, Jameson started the car. "There's a dam on Deer Creek near the reservoir. I promised Nate we could check it out. It's just a short walk from the road."

"Then let's go. There's not much daylight left."

As Nate cheered in the back seat, Jameson pulled out. After days spent so preoccupied with his presence in her life, having him so near in the close confines of the car overloaded her senses. She had to shut her eyes to at least block out the visual if she had any hope of keeping her mind on the straight and narrow.

His scent still infiltrated her awareness—a trace of

the spicy aftershave that had become so familiar, mixed with his male scent. She wanted so much to reach over to him, lay her hand on his arm to feel him, skin against skin. But she kept her hands to herself.

The drone of the car wheels on pavement lulled her and she drifted off during the short drive out to the reservoir. His hand on her shoulder startled her awake, sending her heart rate into overdrive. When she looked over at him, he was only inches away and she nearly raised her hand to caress his face.

"Come on, Mom, we gotta get moving!"

Nate's shout brought her to her senses. She pulled away from Jameson and stepped from the car. Nate squirmed with impatience while Jameson locked the car, then they all headed down the dirt path toward the reservoir.

Nate skipped on ahead of them, still within sight but far enough away to allow private conversation. Nina couldn't help but smile at that slim sturdy body marching along. "You've done so well with him this week, Jameson."

He laughed. "Most of the time I don't know what the hell I'm doing."

"Welcome to the club." She glanced over at him and saw some of the perennial tension in his shoulders release. "Everyone assumes a woman instinctively knows how to mother just because she's female. The first year with him I was so inept, I was convinced I wasn't wired right inside."

He gave her a long look. "Believe me, Nina, everything about you is wired exactly right."

His remark stole her breath. She tore her gaze from

his and tried to put more space between them. But when she edged aside, she caught her toe on a tree root and stumbled. He took her arm to help her rebalance, scrambling her thoughts all over again.

She tugged away and cast about for something to break the taut threads of heat that seemed to bind them together. "I've been trying to remember your mother."

The tightness returned to his shoulders. "Not likely you would. I doubt you were much older than Nate when she died."

"How old were you?"

"Eight." The clipped word didn't invite further inquiry.

Still she pressed on. "It must have been hard on your father."

"My father…" Anger stormed in his face. "He wasn't worth even an ounce of your sympathy."

Up ahead, Nate reached the creek and clambered up on a boulder beside it. He scanned the rippling water. "Where is it, Jameson?"

Jameson left her behind, covering the last several yards with his long-legged stride. Nina hung back.

"It's upstream, Nate." Jameson reached up and Nate jumped from the boulder into his father's arms. Jameson gave him a brief, fierce hug then set him down. "Just a short walk."

He turned back to her then, his expression an enigmatic mix of emotions. Reaching his hand out to her, he transmitted a silent plea. In that moment, she knew he needed her, needed the physical contact of her hand in his.

There was no way to refuse. She closed the gap that separated them and took his hand.

Chapter Eight

Nate's fascination with the beaver dam didn't last long when the occupants refused to make an appearance. He shifted his focus to a fallen log, its underside rotted away, which at Jameson's suggestion doubled for a secret cave. As Nate busied himself with an elaborate fantasy about magicians and enchanted creatures living underground, Jameson and Nina sat watching him from a nearby boulder.

The sun, sinking rapidly toward dusk, sent slanting rays through the trees that dappled the forest floor with light. Nina felt a melancholy rise in her as the world turned toward winter and darker, colder days.

The brooding man beside her didn't help her mood. She was tempted to just leave it be, to let the silence stretch. But for her son's sake, she wanted to know more. "Jameson."

He didn't answer. She risked a hand on his shoulder. "I just wanted to know a little more about your family."

"I don't have a family." He turned to her. "Except you and Nate." She saw his need for confirmation.

"We are," she assured him. "But we're not where you came from. Who you were before."

He shook his head. "It's not worth talking about."

"Nate will want to know some day."

He sighed, then leaned back on his hands, the sinew and muscles of his arms shifting as they supported him. "My father was a bastard." He said the word softly, but it lost none of its rancor. "He was…rough. With my mother. With me."

"Jameson, I'm so sorry."

He seemed to shake off her sympathy. "My mother was…maybe not a saint, but pretty damn close. While she was alive, she was my shield."

Sitting up, he hunched with his hands locked together in his lap. "She never should have married him. She'd come from wealth and could have had anyone. But when she got pregnant, my father smelled the money. He demanded she marry him."

He turned to her, his face as rigid as the granite below them. "Exactly what I did with you." He laughed, a hollow sound. "I hadn't made the connection."

"Your reasons were different," she reminded him. "The two situations are nothing alike."

"Even so…" He let out a long breath. "My mother would tell me he was a good man with a hard life. He wasn't."

He balled his hands tightly. "Apparently he kept his fists to himself until I was born. By then, my mother's family had abandoned her. All that money my father had expected never came."

Nina's heart ached for him. She inched closer and put her arm around his shoulders. He flinched, giving her a wild look. It took him a moment to relax again, accept her contact.

"I don't remember much about her." He gazed off into the trees, as if seeking the memories. "She had dark hair, a little lighter than yours. Blue eyes. A sweet smile." The ropy muscles of his back rippled under her arm. "Every day she'd talk about leaving him. Until she got pregnant again."

In all the old gossip, Nina didn't recall anything about a brother or sister. "I didn't know you had a sibling."

His jaw knotted and tension came off him in waves. "A brother. And my mother…there were complications from the pregnancy. Hemorrhaging. She died a week later."

Wanting to soothe Jameson's agony, she stroked his back. But he didn't acknowledge her touch, didn't respond.

"They came to take my brother." The words seemed torn from him.

"Who?"

"My mother's parents. They took him." His voice turned cold. "But not me."

If there was any trace of that little boy who'd been left behind by his grandparents, Jameson kept it well protected. "Jameson—"

His sharp look cut off anything else she might have said. "They raised him. I stayed with my father until I was eighteen. Joined the Marines. He died while I was in Kuwait."

"Your brother—"

"Dead." He pushed off from the boulder, strode over to Nate. "Time to go, sport." He swung Nate up on his shoulders.

While Nate played at being a giant, aided by Jameson's enthusiastic sound effects, Nina followed behind them on the trail. Jameson had shut her out, using the game with Nate as a diversion.

She tried to piece a story together from what Jameson had told her. She felt slightly ashamed that all through school, she'd been so caught up with her own friends, she had no time for the quiet, sometimes angry loner who didn't seem to fit in anywhere. Then when Jameson had left after high school, she was so madly in love with Tom Jarret she never noticed that the sullen boy with deep brown hair and lost blue eyes was gone.

By the time they reached the car, it was nearly dark and a chill breeze sent a shiver through her. She waited until Jameson had secured Nate's seat belt and shut the door.

"Jameson." She wrapped her arms around herself against the cold. He reached for the door handle. "Jameson," she said again.

He wouldn't meet her gaze, but he didn't open the door. "Yeah."

There were a thousand questions she wanted to ask, but she narrowed her inquiry down to one. "Are your grandparents still alive?"

Shadows shrouded his face, but she heard the reluctance in his voice. "My grandmother is."

"Are you still in touch?"

A long pause, then, "Not exactly."

"Does she know about Nate?"

"No." He wrenched open the door. "Look, it's damn cold out here. I want to get home."

He was inside with the engine started before she'd barely taken her seat. Nina glanced in the back at Nate as she latched her seat belt. Nate had one of the carved wooden cars and was idly spinning the wheels.

Nina lowered her voice. "When are you going to tell her?"

Jameson slammed the car into Reverse and the tires spit gravel as he backed onto the roadway. "I'm not."

"You have to."

The car squealed as he peeled out on the pavement. "I don't."

"She needs to know."

"I'm sure she wouldn't care one way or the other."

The bleakness of his declaration stabbed at her. "How will you know unless you tell her?"

The speedometer edged over the speed limit as he wound his way back toward town. "I'm not telling her, Nina. This is none of your business."

"It's *his* business. And that makes it mine." She stole another quick glance back at Nate, then leaned close to Jameson. "He should know his great-grandmother."

His hands looked ready to tear the steering wheel apart. "No."

"Even if there's bad blood between the two of you—"

"I said no!" He slammed on the brakes and wrenched the car over to the side of the road. The car fishtailed in the dirt of the turnout before it came to a stop. Jameson shoved the car into Park, then pushed out the door.

Rounding the open door, he strode across the path of the headlight beams to the boundary of trees lining the road. As he paced along the edge of the woods, he held his shoulders stiffly against whatever pain roiled inside him.

"Mommy, what's the matter?" Nate's small voice drifted to the front. "How come we stopped?"

"Jameson's checking something. He'll be back in a minute." At least she hoped he would, that he wouldn't just disappear into the trees.

But not more than a few minutes had passed before he returned to the car. Pulling the door shut, he turned the car back onto the road without so much as glancing her way.

Torn between fear of the darkness that inhabited Jameson and a longing to heal the agonizing hurt that cut him so deeply, Nina turned over in her mind what to say to him that would somehow close the rift between them. But words seemed empty useless things that might just as easily wound as they would soothe. So she held her tongue.

But when they pulled up to the house, she realized she didn't need words. She waited until he shut off the engine, before he could escape the confined space of the car. Catching his hand, she brought it to her lips and pressed a kiss to his palm.

Then she pitched her voice low so Nate wouldn't hear. "I would have never left you behind."

It shouldn't have meant so damn much to him.

The hurts of more than twenty years ago were buried in the past and too much had happened in between to give them much meaning anymore. The knife wound in his side from his first year in Folsom was fresher than the ancient pain inflicted by his grandmother, and something far more worthy of Nina's sympathy.

Monday didn't turn out at all as he had hoped with a day off for him and Nina, and Nate busy with his field trip. The foreman had left a message on their answering machine Sunday night that a pipe fitting had burst in one of the bathrooms on the job site and some cabinetry had to be torn out to repair it. He wanted Jameson in on Monday to reinstall the cabinetry.

It had only taken a half-day of work to finish the job and the foreman promised him either overtime or a day off, his choice. So he had next Monday to look forward to with Nina. And this afternoon, or at least the two or three hours before Nate returned.

When he pulled up the drive, she was out in the front yard, raking oak leaves from the grass. She wore a pair of pale blue jeans that looked soft and worn and a rose-colored V-neck sweater that shaped the tempting curves of her full breasts. She'd tied her hair back with ribbon and the early afternoon sun tinted her creamy cheeks with shades of gold.

God, he wanted to touch her. As he eased from the car, his own jeans uncomfortably tight from his body's response to her, he didn't know how long he'd be able to keep his hands off her. As much as he'd looked forward to time alone with her, it would be an agony to keep himself from pulling her into his arms.

He reached in the back seat for his tool belt, buying time to get himself under control. But when he turned back to her, saw her welcoming smile, he realized it had been a futile effort. He would have to be dead to keep from responding to her.

He crossed the lawn toward her. "Give me a minute to put this away and I'll give you a hand."

She smoothed her hair back behind her ear and he wanted to trace that same path with his fingers. "I'm nearly finished. I've just been waiting for you." Her soft-spoken comment ran over him like a caress. "I picked up the paint for the playroom."

Painting wasn't top of his list of activities he'd like to be engaged in with Nina, but as long as he was spending time with her, he'd take it as a second choice. He'd gotten the prep work done on the room Saturday night and now it was ready for a coat of white paint.

By the time he'd taken the tool belt into the service porch and returned outside, she had a black trash bag open and was trying to scoop the leaves into the bag. As she leaned over, the vee of her sweater gapped and gave him an enticing glimpse of the tops of her breasts. He should have looked away, but his gaze lingered.

When she lifted her soft brown eyes and caught him staring, he saw such an answering heat in her gaze that his hunger for her tripled. He let himself look his fill before reaching for the bag.

"I'll hold it for you." There was no hiding the raw need in his voice. "You rake them in."

Warmth seemed to radiate from her, an aura of sexuality she couldn't have concealed even if she'd dressed herself in the black trash bag. As she worked, her special fragrance—a fragment of something floral mixed with something womanly and uniquely Nina—curled around him in a sensual haze. The crunch of the leaves, their own musky scent combining with the smokiness of autumn, made his desire almost painful.

She'd barely raked in the last of the leaves when he yanked the bag shut and tied the top. Tossing it aside, he took the rake from Nina and dropped it on the lawn. A hand on her shoulder, he urged her closer until he could see the passion in her wide dark eyes.

As he bent his head closer, her lips parted. Her breath caressed his mouth as he brushed her lips with his. The heat of her, the sweet taste he knew waited for him, jolted through him like a lightning bolt. His body shook with anticipation.

He slipped his tongue inside her mouth and thought he would fall apart right there. He let himself drink from her, explore the mysteries of her mouth for only a few moments. Then he knew he had to get her inside or he would embarrass them both on their front lawn. Their home was off the beaten path, but there was no guarantee a neighbor wouldn't drop by to say hello. They couldn't risk it.

He bent and picked her up, one arm hooked behind her knees, the other around her shoulders. He'd carried her this way yesterday, but then he'd had good intentions—to put her to bed for much-needed rest. Today was a different story. He wanted her in *his* bed, her lush curves pressed against him, her tantalizing, silky heat all his.

He'd promised her a marriage in name only, that they could share a house without sharing a bed. He hesitated in the kitchen, let her down although he still held her tight against him. "We don't have to," he whispered harshly, although his body screamed a different message. "I can let you go right now."

Despite his vow, he wasn't sure he could. She didn't test him, instead reached up to pull him down to her, her soft full lips claiming his, her tongue tentatively pushing inside his mouth. He groaned, again on the edge of exploding. Dragging in a breath, he fought the rising fire.

Hands cupping her hips, he lifted her onto a kitchen stool and stepped between her legs. Her back against the butcher-block island, he thrust against the vee of her legs. Her moan seared through him, pulverizing reason, leaving behind elemental sexual need. Nearing the point of no return, he drew back, gave himself breathing space.

When she would have pulled him closer, he brought his hand up over her breast and lightly stroked her through the sweater. Her nipple beaded against his palm and he teased it, reveling in the sound of hunger whispering from her lips. He wanted desperately to bring her to climax, to experience again what he had that incandescent night when he gloried in her passion. He wanted her release even more fervently than his own.

Letting his hand drift down, he edged under the hem of her sweater. She moaned, whether in protest or encouragement, he wasn't sure. It didn't matter; he wanted to feel her against his hand, explore her most intimate places.

Her breath caught as he released the button of her jeans and slowly lowered the zipper. His fingers grazed lightly along the satiny knit of her panties, then at her waist, dipped underneath. She writhed against him, her hand wrapping around his wrist. He stopped, waited. Then her fingers loosened and fell away. Slowly, lazily, he stroked lower.

At the first bleat of the telephone, he stopped his

downward exploration, but kept his fingers in tantalizing motion. "Should I answer it?" he murmured against her neck, although he felt pretty sure of her answer.

Eyes half-lidded, she lolled back against his arm, her hair mussed and drifting loose from the ribbon. "The machine can pick it up."

He untied the ribbon and set it aside, then let her hair fall across his palm. A delicate scent tickled his nose. Maybe after they finished making love, he'd brush her hair, explore its fragrant silk.

"Here?" he asked, his fingers teasing again. "Or my room?"

Behind him the phone stopped ringing and the answering machine clicked in. As he backed his way through the kitchen toward his bedroom, the machine's beep sounded. There was a hesitation, as if the caller had changed their mind about leaving a message, then the woman spoke.

"Nina? It's Lydia Heath." The cultured tones sent ice through Jameson's veins. "I'm sorry I missed you. Please call back. I'd like to talk."

He felt Nina's gaze on him as he put her away from him. He couldn't look at her as he struggled to trap his anger inside him. If he let it out—he didn't want Nina to see that kind of rage, the nightmare storm his father had unleashed on his mother so many times.

A roaring filled his ears and he only dimly heard the woman on the phone leave her number. He vaguely registered the area code as that of the high-rent community of Palo Alto, but before the machine clicked off, he was on his way out the door. He never heard the last few words of his grandmother's goodbye.

* * *

Nina fumbled with the zipper of her jeans, shame scalding her cheeks. When Jameson was touching her, she'd been exultant, overwhelmed with a soul-deep joy. She was eager to give herself to him, to have him inside her, to join with him intimately.

She retrieved the ribbon from the island and hurried out the front door. As she tied her hair back again, she saw the Camry retreating down the drive toward the road. The tires screeched as Jameson gunned it toward town.

Shoulders sagging, she returned to the house. It had been a calculated risk calling Jameson's grandmother on his behalf. Although she'd known he would be angry, she hadn't expected this much rage.

But despite Jameson's reaction, she knew it had been the right thing to do. So far in his short life, Nate had been cut off from half his family. Until Jameson had returned, she'd been able to justify to herself her rationale for keeping Nate ignorant of his father's roots. But now she'd accepted Jameson into Nate's life, opening a door that had to include Jameson's grandmother.

She checked the kitchen clock and saw she still had an hour before one of the parent chaperones from the preschool dropped off Nate. She might as well get a start on the painting she'd hoped to do with Jameson.

By the time she heard the sound of a car door slamming, she'd nearly finished the roller work on all four walls, leaving just brush work near floor and ceiling and around the door, closet and window. Another car door slammed as she poured the leftover paint from the roller tray back into the can and she assumed the parent chaperone was walking Nate to the front door. Grabbing a paper towel as she detoured into the kitchen, she quickly wiped wet paint from her hands.

Before she could reach it, the front door opened. Nate raced inside, a stuffed tiger clutched to his chest, and made a beeline for the bathroom. Nina smiled, ready to greet the mom or dad who had escorted Nate inside. But it was Jameson who entered behind Nate.

He shut the door behind him. "I got back just as he arrived."

Dirt smudged the front of his white T-shirt and bits of sawdust speckled his jeans. Earlier she'd been too caught up in holding him, touching him, to notice the evidence of a hard morning's work. His sigh, the hand he ran over his face, told her how tired he must be. He'd only put in a few hours today, but all week he'd been working his job and helping her with hers. Her actions today, no matter how well-intentioned, had driven him away before he could even change out of his work clothes.

Nevertheless, they both had to face the issue. She gripped the wadded paper towel tightly in her hand. "We have to talk."

She could see he wanted to refuse, but he gave her a brusque nod. She would have said something more, but by then Nate had returned, eager to show off his tiger, then the excitement of his day spilled out. She felt Jameson's intense gaze occasionally on her even as he smiled at Nate's recital and prompted him with questions.

When Nate finally ran out of steam, he trotted off to his room to introduce his tiger to his carved wooden cars. Alone with Jameson, Nina tried to think what to do next even as she had to discipline herself against reaching up to touch his cheek.

He spoke first. "Can you get your parents to watch Nate tonight?"

She nodded. "I'll call them."

"There's a Mexican place in Marbleville. Their food is pretty good."

"Nate and I have had dinner there." The air between them crackled despite the banality of their conversation. "We like it."

"I'll go change, then." He hesitated, leaned toward her as if he intended to close the distance between them. Then he turned and headed for his room.

Nina felt a chill, as if autumn had crept into the room. She wished she could put her arms around Jameson, take in his heat. At the same time her feelings for him confused and frightened her. He was a stranger, but a stranger with whom she had the most intimate history.

Shaking herself from her reverie, she picked up the kitchen phone and quickly dialed her parents' house. Her mother was delighted to have Nate over for the evening and even offered to let him spend the night. She and Nina's father could drop him off at the preschool before they drove down to Sacramento for the day.

Nate was over the moon with excitement at spending the night at his grandma's house. Any guilt Nina might have had over neglecting her son on her one day off was washed away with his enthusiasm. She helped him load up his backpack with pajamas, a change of clothes, toothbrush and a few picture books. With the backpack by the front door and the stuffed tiger beside it, Nina headed for her bathroom for her own shower.

As she stood in front of her closet brushing back her wet hair, Nina couldn't remember the last time she'd worn a dress. *Tres Amigos* wasn't a fancy place, but it would be such a treat to get a little "gussied up," as her mother would say. She realized she wanted to look nice for Jameson as well, to have him see her in something more feminine than jeans or her plain black work slacks.

She pulled a cornflower-blue cashmere sweaterdress from the back of the closet and held it out. Its scoop neckline barely clung to her shoulders, requiring a strapless bra, but she'd always felt so pretty wearing it. The long sleeves would keep her warm enough against the coolness of the autumn evening and the wide black, patent leather belt accentuated her figure.

After donning panty hose and a strapless bra, she tugged on the dress, a little afraid it wouldn't fit after all these years. But although the dress clung to every curve, one glance in the mirror assured her she looked every bit as feminine as she remembered in the smoky blue knit. Slipping into low black pumps, she found a pair of onyx earrings her mother had given her. A little work with the blow-dryer to style her hair and she was finished.

She transferred a few things from her everyday bag into a small black patent leather purse, then stepped from her room. Taking a breath, she headed up the carpeted hall toward the living room. Suddenly nervous and shy, she paused just short of the end of the hall and peeked inside.

Jameson was kneeling, speaking to Nate, his back to her. He wore charcoal gray slacks that fit neatly on his slim hips. He'd rolled up the sleeves of his pale gray dress shirt and the fine weave stretched tautly across his broad shoulders. His dark hair, still a bit damp from his shower, barely brushed his collar.

Gathering courage, she stepped inside the room and Nate smiled up at her. "You look pretty, Mommy."

Jameson straightened, turning toward her. His stunned expression said everything, turning her hot and cold all at once. She wanted so much to be in his arms, to have him hold her. But there was too much standing between them—the ugliness of his past, which still haunted him, her own reluctance to give herself to a man she didn't know at all.

How much of that they might clear away at dinner, she didn't know. But at least tonight she could be pretty for him. She could be a woman he would be proud to have at his side. The rest they could work through later.

Chapter Nine

After their encounter this afternoon, Nina could have appeared in a burlap sack and still aroused him to a fever pitch. The dress she wore, soft blue knit that begged him to touch, sent his nerve endings into overload. He could barely think straight with her sitting across the restaurant table from him, let alone focus clearly enough to order dinner. The menu might as well be in Aramaic instead of its mix of Spanish and English.

He picked something almost at random, then once the waitress left, he slid his water toward himself and gulped down half the glass. The ice water sent a chill through him and he was tempted to dump the remainder on his head to finish the job of dampening his lust. Instead he set the glass back on the table and wiped his hands dry on his paper napkin.

Nina lifted her gaze to his, her expression serious. "About your grandmother…"

That introduction was twice as effective as a bucket of ice water. Jameson set aside his crumpled napkin. "Yeah?"

Her lips pursed with irritation at his unhelpful obtuseness. He just wanted to kiss them. Her dark eyes flashed. "You agreed to talk about this."

He had, although he'd just as soon his grandmother disappear off the face of the earth. "What do you want from me, Nina?" He knew the answer, but couldn't seem to suppress a perverse urge to stall.

"I want Nate to meet her."

He forced himself to relax his jaw. "She's not someone I want around my son."

"When she left you behind…maybe she thought your brother could adapt because he was a baby. But you were older and to pull you from your home—"

Indignation burned like acid in the pit of his stomach. "She knew what kind of man my father was."

"Did she? Have you ever asked her about it?" She saw the answer in his face. "Maybe it's time you made peace with her. Maybe it's time you let go of the past."

"The past made me what I am now." The words seemed to strafe his throat as he spoke them. "The past is what sent me to prison."

He saw the flash of fear in her soft eyes at the reminder. Knowing Nina, she'd persuaded herself to block his manslaughter conviction from her mind. How else could she live with him? Allow him near her son?

He could have cleared away that fear with just a handful of words, an easily spoken assurance. The truth wouldn't frighten her as much as his reputation did. He wanted her to understand the extent of his grandmother's sin, and he might be able to bolster his case with the truth more than he could by lying about the rumors. But he hated giving his grandmother any credit for his redemption.

Nina reached across the table and gripped his hand. "No matter what you think of her, or how much you hate her, Nate deserves a chance to meet her—to get to know her on his own terms. If she's as cruel as you say she is, he'll find out soon enough."

He wanted to turn his hand, lock his fingers with hers. That connection might heal some of the wounds that still throbbed deep within him. But he needed to heal himself, not expect Nina to do it for him.

His agreement stuck in his throat, but he forced it out. "She can meet him."

She smiled and he would have leaped to the moon in that moment if she'd asked it. He still would rather have had his teeth pulled without Novocain than introduce Nate to Lydia Heath, but Nina's smile at least made the intolerable bearable.

The waitress approached from the kitchen with their dinner plates and Nina pulled her hand away. As the young woman set the hot food before them, Nina arranged her napkin on her lap. Her upper arms pushed against her breasts, deepening her cleavage and drawing Jameson's gaze inexorably to that bewitching mystery.

If he'd never touched her, the fantasy of cupping her with his hands would be tantalizing enough. But he had caressed her there, had brushed his palms against her nipples and reveled in the weight of her soft flesh. That tipped the fantasy into memory and that much closer to reality.

With an effort, he bent his head to his food and forced himself to eat. Beef with a red sauce so spicy his eyes watered, rice and frijoles topped with cheese. He took a flour tortilla from the warmer and rolled a healthy helping of the beef into it. The scalding piquancy of the sauce redirected his straying thoughts and sent him grabbing for his water glass again.

Nina cut neat bites of her enchilada, her wide mouth opening to take a forkful. Jameson kept his head down, unwilling to think about her lips.

She set down her fork. "When?"

Jameson struggled with the question. When what? If it had anything to do with covering her mouth with his, he was right on it. Then he remembered their previous, unpleasant conversation. He took another bite of tortilla and beef ranchero. "I don't know." He reached for his glass but he'd already emptied it.

"We could have her down for Thanksgiving at my folks' house."

Jameson tried to imagine haughty, blue-blooded Lydia at the same table as Nina's warm, openhearted parents. An impossible image. His grandmother would take one snooty look at the Russo's plain table setting and modest home and make her disapproval clear. That there was more love displayed in that house than Lydia ever showed for her daughter or grandson wouldn't figure into his grandmother's disdain.

The busboy arrived to refill his glass. A swallow of water delayed Jameson's answer. "I don't think Thanksgiving would work."

Nina pinned him with her frank gaze. "Will anything work to your satisfaction?"

He could see she wouldn't let the issue rest until he'd made a commitment. Groping for a remotely palatable solution, he sighed with relief when the bleat of Nina's cell phone saved him.

As she retrieved the phone from her purse, the instant worry in her face mirrored his own—had something happened to Nate? The Russos would protect their grandson better than the Secret Service did the president, but he was a lively little boy and anything could happen even in the most vigilant care.

"Nate?" Jameson asked, then let out a gust of air when Nina shook her head.

As she listened to the caller, she sagged back in her chair with a sigh. Whatever news she was receiving over the phone, it wasn't good.

She rolled her eyes once, then shook her head. When she finally spoke, Jameson could hear the faint irritation in her voice. "If that's what you want, Dale. Best of luck to you."

The corners of her mouth turned down, she switched off the phone and tucked it into her purse. Jameson captured her hand across the table. "What was that all about?"

"Dale. The night cook." Frank disbelief marked her face. "He's moving to Reno. He wants to be a boxman at the craps table."

Jameson would have laughed if he didn't know what a disaster that was for Nina. "He never was very dedicated."

"No, but at least he was there."

"Most of the time."

She rubbed at her brow in agitation. "What am I going to do for a cook?"

The answer came easily. "I'll do it."

"What?"

He squeezed her hand. "I'll take over as cook."

This was turning into a nightmare. Dale leaving her high and dry—although she'd expected it sooner or later, it was still a shock—and Jameson offering to take his place. She already struggled enough with crazy mixed feelings about Jameson, which had ratcheted up even higher after this afternoon's steamy interlude. His constant presence at the café would drive her mad.

She tugged her hand free, the contact too distracting. "You can't work your job all day then cook at night."

"There's only another week of work at the housing development. I'd be scouting around for another job then anyway."

Despite her desperation, she had to find a way to deflect Jameson's offer. "A cook's salary wouldn't be half what you're paid as a cabinetry man."

"I don't need the cook's salary."

"The mortgage—"

"I can cover it."

With that mysterious source of money he wouldn't discuss. She'd run out of excuses and fell back on the truth. Fingers locked together in her lap, she let the confession slip out. "I don't know if I can work with you."

She was grateful he didn't pretend to misunderstand. "I won't touch you, Nina."

She felt heat rise to her face as she whispered, "You don't have to."

His blue eyes darkened and she thought she might ignite on the spot. She wished he'd look away, but he kept his gaze on her. "I know. But we can do this. Please, Nina. It would mean a lot to me."

She remembered how he had been five years ago when he'd worked in the café. He'd seemed like a different person then from the sad sullen boy she'd known in school. He'd been happy, content. Performing what some would consider the most menial of jobs, he'd seemed to flower. For that short golden time, they'd been a family to him.

So he wanted that back. How could she refuse him?

She nodded cautiously. "Okay. We can do it."

He smiled, and the uncharacteristic softening of his face, his eyes, sent a melting heat through her. "Good. That's good."

Lowering her gaze, she picked up her fork again. "Dale's giving me three more days. I won't need you until Friday."

"Fine. I'll let the foreman know."

She wasn't inclined to finish her now cold enchiladas, but the alternative—spending the evening home alone with Jameson—didn't bear thinking about. Picking at the rest of her meal as Jameson took a few desultory bites of his own, she wished she could teleport herself into her room with her door safely padlocked.

Jameson set down his fork and glanced at his watch. "We could try to catch a film."

The Marbleville Six was just another block over. An appealing prospect—it would delay their return home by a couple of hours. She sighed. "Not tonight. I'm opening tomorrow. I need to get to bed."

She didn't have to be a clairvoyant to read what flashed through his mind—he wanted to be there with her. She wanted the same thing and how she'd resist letting him join her there without the excuse of her son to stand between them she didn't know.

Crossing her arms over her middle, she hugged herself tightly, as if that would hold the hot, insistent urges in. His gaze dropped to her cleavage only for a moment before he raised it to a more polite perusal of her face. But he didn't need to be looking at her breasts to make it clear he wanted to put his hands on them. And she remembered all too clearly what that felt like, the exquisite pleasure of it.

She gasped in a breath. "We should go."

Jameson grabbed the check and headed for the register to pay. Purse in hand, Nina rose on shaky legs and joined him. His fingers on the small of her back, he escorted her from the restaurant.

Thick silence filled the car on the drive home. Nina wanted to scream, to cry, to ask him to pull the Camry over so she could devour him. By the time they pulled up to the house, she felt like a wreck.

Without turning off the engine, Jameson climbed from the car and walked with her to the front porch. She glanced from him to the car. "What—"

"I'm going for a drive." He didn't move from the porch and she knew he waited for her to either agree or to ask him to stay with her.

Her choice. Safety or wild sensuality. He was ready to accept the former or indulge the latter.

Her mother had always told her she was a good, sensible girl. Her one lapse with Jameson notwithstanding, Pauline Russo had been right about her daughter.

And even now, when torn between the clamoring of

her body and the sure thing of a night alone, she couldn't seem to avoid that little voice inside that instructed her to take the proper path. It was only what she and Jameson had agreed to when they'd married. But somehow, even as she made her choice, she felt like a coward.

"I'd better get inside then," she told him. "It'll be great to get a full night's sleep."

There was no judgment as he nodded and brushed a kiss on her brow. He hesitated long enough to see her safely inside, then she heard his footsteps descending the stairs. Nudging aside the living room curtains, she watched temptation drive away.

She supposed it was just desserts that when she finally climbed in bed, she couldn't sleep a wink until she heard his car return.

Despite the never-ending edge of sexual tension between them, Nina discovered she enjoyed having Jameson working with her in the café. She could let go of the nagging anxiety she carried around every day wondering if she'd have a night cook. Jameson she could count on. She might not know much else about the man she'd bound herself to, but she was certain of his commitment to the café.

With Jameson there in the evenings, Nina could take Nate home in the afternoons and spend a few precious hours with him. She'd make enough dinner for three, then take Jameson's share over to the café. She and Nate would sit with him after the dinner rush, talk and exchange tidbits about their day while he ate.

The Sunday before Thanksgiving, Nina sent Nate back to his cubby to watch a video so she and Jameson could talk alone. The café was closed and most of the cleanup already completed. Nina waited until Jameson finished the last of his brisket and gravy.

"Your grandmother called again."

In the midst of swabbing his plate with his roll, his hand faltered. He glanced up at her, then ate the bite of bread. Washing it down with ice water, he set his glass carefully on the table.

"Jameson, I can't keep putting her off." When he started to rise from the table, Nina grabbed his hands. "Wait."

A moment's resistance, then he settled back in the booth. He wouldn't meet her gaze and she thought he might still be contemplating escape. But he only broke contact long enough to push the dishes aside. Then he gathered her hands in his, releasing his nervous energy my stroking the backs of her hands with his thumbs.

His touch left her breathless and she had to struggle to speak. "When can we see her?"

He stared down at their linked hands. "Can you get a backup cook the weekend of the trade show?"

His sudden change of subject cramped her already laboring brain. "I guess so." Every December, she or her parents had made an annual pilgrimage to the big restaurant trade show in San Francisco. "I can check with Andrea."

"Nate and I will go with you. On the way there we'll stop by my grandmother's in Palo Alto."

"Good." She smiled at him. "I'll call her."

"No. I will."

She could see from the set of his face that contacting his grandmother was the last thing he wanted to do. But she knew he'd follow through.

"It's time we told Nate," Nina said.

"Yeah."

"You want me—"

"No. We both will." He rose from his seat, then helped her up from hers. Pulling her into his arms, he released a heavy sigh. "I don't want him to like her. How childish is that?"

She tipped her head back to meet his gaze. "Will you let him?"

"I have to." He meted out the words begrudgingly.

"Will you let him love her?"

Anger flickered in his face and he looked away a moment. The only sign of agreement was his curt nod.

Slipping from his arms, Nina took his hand and led him to the back of the café. Nate's interest in a much-watched video had apparently waned. He'd pulled out his crayons and was coloring a picture.

He grinned when they stepped into his cubby. "Look, Mommy. A picture of our family." Five crude stick figures stood beside a mammoth house. "Here's you and me, Grandma and Papa and Daddy."

She felt the shock go through Jameson. His stunned expression squeezed at her heart. His throat worked as he swallowed. "Would you…" he managed.

So she knelt to eye level with Nate and told him about his Great-grandma Lydia and how they'd be visiting her in a few weeks. As she expected, he bounced with excitement at the news; to Nate, grandparents meant special times and plenty of candy and toys. She considered informing him that things might be different with Great-grandma Lydia, but decided it would be best if he found out on his own. Nina didn't know the woman other than their few, brief phone conversations. She didn't want to prejudge her.

As they completed the last few chores to close up, Jameson was still thunderstruck by Nate's casual reference to him as Daddy. Nina searched her own heart for any resentment or jealousy over Nate's acceptance of his father. But she could find only joy there.

Jameson gave Nate his good-night kiss, patted the stuffed white tiger and switched off the light as he left the room. He expected that Nina would already be in bed, but as he passed the kitchen he saw her seated at the butcher-block island.

She smiled, and sensation shot clear to his toes. "I made some herbal tea. Would you like some?"

He laughed, imagining the reaction of his cell mate to him drinking herbal tea. "I'll just nuke the leftover coffee from this morning." He grabbed the pot from the coffeemaker and poured the cold, oily brew into a mug. Setting the mug in the microwave, he paced beside the island, edgy energy prickling along his skin.

The words burst out of him. "He called me *Daddy*."

Nina's sweet look heightened the electricity inside him. "Yes."

"You don't mind?" The microwave beeped and he pulled the mug of coffee from it. It sloshed on his hand. "You're his mom, but I—"

"You've been a good father to him."

The compliment should have pleased him, but instead his stomach churned. "I haven't done anything."

"You have, Jameson. You've done more than you know."

He took a gulp of the coffee, scalding his mouth. "I make his lunch in the mornings, take him to preschool. That's it."

"You play games with him." She rose and moved toward him. "You help him with his letters and numbers."

"Because I'm copying you. I don't know what I'm doing."

"But you do it." She took his hand. "And that's what matters to Nate."

He didn't understand the emotions tightening inside him like a fist. Nina's assurances should have made him happy, but all he could feel was disaster hanging on his shoulders. He might have done it right so far, but sooner or later he'd screw up. Sooner or later something would trip him up, he'd do something wrong, something bad, and Nate would come to hate him. And he wouldn't be Daddy anymore.

He felt Nina's hand on his arm, holding tight. He realized she was calling his name. Still caught up with his sense of doom, he looked down at her, saw only worry in her dark brown eyes. Despite her caring, despite her concern, he felt trapped, confined by the expectation that he knew how to be a father. He knew nothing, had only been pretending all along.

His hand moving with jerky awkwardness, he pulled away from Nina and dropped the mug in the sink with a clatter. Wiping spilled coffee from his hand on the back of his jeans, he slipped past her. "Need some sleep," he said, heading for his room.

"Jameson—"

He didn't turn around. He barreled down the hallway to his room, then prowled the space trying to figure out what to do next. The crazy thoughts rolling over in his head screamed at him to leave, to escape, even while his heart wanted nothing more than to return to the sanctuary of Nina's arms. Images of the past spun like fun house images in his mind—his father's anger, his daddy's fists. Bruises, pain, shameful tears. Him calling out, *Daddy, Daddy, stop!*

He slapped the heels of his palms over his ears, trying to quell the memories. The groan that spilled from his mouth sounded as if something else had uttered it— an animal, something in terrible agony. He had to escape, he had to get away, he had to—

When he first felt Nina's touch, he jolted in fear and wrenched away. But she followed him, her voice soothing, calming, stroking him as surely as her hands caressing his back. She was like a talisman guiding him back from the dark place that had engulfed him. He couldn't understand what she was saying, felt only warmth and comfort in her touch. He didn't even know how long she stood there holding him, didn't even remember when she guided him to his bed and urged him to lie down on it.

Even then she didn't let him go. She stretched out beside him, her body soft and yielding, her adamantine will all the protection he would ever need.

As sleep tugged at him, he puzzled over the notion that Nina would protect him instead of the other way around. Emotions and feelings were a woman's territory. Men controlled what they could, ignored what they couldn't. But Nina had known he was close to drowning.

He woke once during the night and reached for her, but she'd gone off to her own bed. He only dimly recalled the waking nightmare, could remember only that Nina had rescued him from the dark. That was enough to soothe him back into sleep.

Chapter Ten

As they pulled out of Marbleville just past noon and onto Interstate 80, Nina wondered if the entire trip to Palo Alto would pass in silence. After a quick stop for a fill-up and a bathroom break for Nate, even Jameson's monosyllabic responses to her attempts at conversation had ceased. Nate, ensconced in the back seat with a story on CD and read-along book in his lap, wouldn't be offering up his usual chatter.

Thanksgiving at her parents' house had been strangely subdued. It had been a smaller crowd than usual this year, with all but one of Nina's cousins spending the day with their spouses' families. As a consequence, Nate was the only youngster and had been sorely disappointed to have no one to play with.

After Jameson's emotional crisis the Sunday before, Nina was worried he would refuse to go with her to Thanksgiving dinner. But he surprised her by insisting on baking a pecan pie and making sure Nate was properly spiffed up for the occasion. Then, when her father offered up the turkey carving duties to Jameson, he readily accepted. He took the gentle probing questions from her aunts, uncles and cousin in good spirit, answering them as best he could. Her parents must have forewarned the relatives about Jameson's time at Folsom, because that was one topic they skirted entirely.

In the week and a half after Thanksgiving, they resumed their comfortable routine, working as a team to run the café and care for Nate. But as the weekend of the trade show grew nearer, Jameson grew quieter, as if the prospect of seeing his grandmother again had constrained his voice into silence. He might have accepted introducing Lydia Heath to Nate, but it was obvious he still resisted accepting the woman herself.

Nina had tucked a mystery novel and a couple of restaurant trade magazines she'd been meaning to get to in her overnight bag. She supposed she could ask Jameson to pull over so she could retrieve them. But she'd prefer to get Jameson talking, to release some of the tension brewing inside him.

She laid her hand on his arm, felt the rock-hard muscles under the sleeve of his gray wool sweater. When she rubbed gently, trying to soothe, he flicked a glance to her before returning his attention to the road. She felt his arm relax infinitesimally.

"Have you been to your grandmother's house before?"

His muscles tightened again. "Once."

"When was that?" she prompted.

"Long time ago."

His perfunctory responses sent a trace of irritation up

her spine. "Jameson, talk to me. I know you hate this, that visiting your grandmother is the last thing you want to do. But we've decided. We're doing it. So let's talk it out."

Faint color rose in his face. "Fine. We'll talk."

She stroked the taut muscles of his arm. "This is tough for you."

He let out a long breath. "Yeah." A big rig slowed in front of them and Jameson moved into the passing lane. "I only met my grandmother once…the day she and my grandfather came to take my brother."

"But you've been to her house."

He nodded. "When I was seven or so. I didn't see her that day." His hands gripped the wheel, then loosened. "My mother was pregnant with my brother. My father was gone for a few days…up to Reno, maybe? My mother borrowed a car and drove up to Palo Alto."

Traffic thickened as they neared Sacramento. Jameson passed another trucker. "My grandfather wouldn't even let my mother in. She stood there, I don't know how many months pregnant and he screamed at her on the front porch. Some of the names he called her…" His jaw knotted. "My own father was a bastard, but my grandfather…I remember thinking he was evil. God, he scared me."

"But he's gone, now."

"Thank God. While I was at Folsom."

"Then the day they took your brother…"

He didn't answer right away, too busy navigating the labyrinth of freeway exchanges in Sacramento. When he'd settled into a lane on Interstate 80 west, he finally spoke. "They were both there that day."

He raked back his hair with his fingers. "She didn't say much. When my grandfather demanded my father hand over my brother, I remember my grandmother looking at me. I was so crushed by my mother's death, most of that day was a blur. But I do remember her looking at me. And when my father told them they better take me if they were taking the baby, she opened her mouth, like she was about to say something. But then my grandfather handed her my brother and they walked out."

"You've never talked with her since?"

"Until I called to arrange this visit." His expression hardened. "I never wanted to."

What seemed so clear to her Jameson would not even consider. "It might not have been her decision to leave you behind."

"It doesn't matter. When she didn't speak up for me, it might as well have been her decision."

"We can't do anything to change the past, Jameson." Still, Nina felt compelled to do something about the future, despite the impossibility of it. "None of it matters now. It's ancient history. We're starting fresh, today, right now."

He didn't respond, just kept his gaze on the traffic lane in front of him. She squeezed his arm. "Will you give it a chance? Put the past aside—"

His fierce look cut her off. Anger bubbled just beneath the surface. He turned back to the road.

"Just consider it, Jameson. If your grandfather frightened you, he might have terrified your grandmother just as much. Enough to force her to leave behind an eight-year-old boy she would have rather taken with her."

She saw the moment the possibility burst beneath the

surface of the impenetrable shell around Jameson's heart. He still didn't speak, but insight lit his face, softened its edges.

They continued on in an easier silence, the Camry eating up the miles between Sacramento and Palo Alto. Her heart a shade lighter, Nina leaned back in her seat and let the drone of the wheels ease her into sleep.

As Nina dozed beside him, Jameson struggled to keep his focus on his driving. He felt more shell-shocked by Nina's insight than he had the first day he stepped inside Folsom Prison. He'd spent decades with hatred for his grandparents burning away inside him, his vitriol narrowing on Lydia Heath after his grandfather's death. With his few scattered encounters with his grandparents, he'd never tried to put the pieces into place— his grandmother may have been just as cowed as his own mother by a tyrant. His anger all these years might have been entirely misplaced.

If he'd known…but how would that have changed anything? Would he have had the means to pull his brother from his grandparents' house? His grandfather had been an influential, high-powered CEO, a man with more money than virtue. By the time Jameson was old enough to stand up to Garret Heath, his brother, Sean, was already set on his dark path. The die had already been cast, and the headlong chain of events still would have landed Jameson in prison.

Still, he might have had more empathy for his grandmother once the old man had died. His gratitude for her help in securing his release from Folsom might have been easier to bear. He'd always assumed that she'd been part and parcel of his grandfather's cruel rejection of his mother, and later, himself. If she'd been too intimidated to resist…

He couldn't change the past, just as Nina had said. But he could begin to let go of the sharp pieces of bitterness he'd let lodge inside him for far too long. He still felt resentment that his grandmother hadn't stood up to his grandfather…but his own mother had accepted his father's fists. He could understand that kind of fear, could even work toward forgiving it.

And maybe, despite the anger that still rooted deep inside him, maybe he could forgive Lydia Heath. He'd done everything he could to shape himself into a different kind of man than his own father had been. What would show greater strength than to absolve Lydia Heath of the transgressions of her husband?

Jameson had hinted at the kind of wealth his mother had come from. But when Nina got her first look at the Heaths' palatial estate, she was astounded. An Italian villa transported to the Bay Area, the two-story home had a triple arched portico, creamy stucco walls and clay tile roof. Palm trees and native oaks surrounded the home and a double set of stairs climbed to a landing that spanned the front of the villa. A concrete ramp, its slope more gentle than the stairs, curved up the knoll as well.

Nina took in the vast tree-studded grounds. "I had no idea you could find this much land in the Bay Area."

Jameson pulled the car up to the foot of the stairs. "It was built back in 1913 by my great-great-grandfather."

Nina caught a glimpse of a slender, white-haired woman waiting on the portico. A man in a severe black suit began descending the left-hand stairs. Nina sent Jameson a questioning look.

A ghost of a smile curved his lips. "I'm guessing that's the butler."

Jameson brushed a finger across her cheek, then climbed from the car. Nina followed suit. Nate had already hopped from the back seat.

He stared up at the mammoth house. "Wowsers."

The butler had reached the bottom of the stairs. With his spare frame, cropped salt-and-pepper hair and sharp, angular face, he could have been anywhere from thirty to fifty. "Mr. O'Connell? Can I help you with your luggage?"

"We're staying in the city." The coolness of Jameson's tone was clear. "We won't need our luggage."

The butler nodded, then turned back toward the stairs. "This way, please."

Nina wondered why Lydia hadn't come down to greet them herself. After her conversations with the woman, Nina came away with the impression that she was a kind and genuine person. She certainly didn't seem the type to put on airs because she was wealthy.

After being pent up in the car for two and a half hours, Nate raced up the stairs ahead of them. By the time Nina and Jameson reached the top with the butler, Nate had already approached his great-grandmother. Lydia, face-to-face with her great-grandson for the first time, avidly drank in every detail, a look of joy in her faded blue eyes.

Now Nina saw why she hadn't come down the stairs herself. She gripped a walker tightly, her wrist joints gnarled and swollen, her hips awkwardly uneven. But in that moment, any awareness of her physical disability was surely swept away by her elation at seeing Nate.

Nina hung back, and a hand on Jameson's arm kept him beside her. Nate swaggered up to Lydia, sturdy and pugnacious as he stood before her. "Hi, I'm Nate. Are you my great-grandmother?"

Lydia beamed, her smile lighting her weathered face. "I am, young man."

Nate tapped the front of the aluminum walker. "What's this for?"

Nina bit back a chastisement as Lydia leaned down toward Nate a bit. "It helps me walk. My legs don't work as well as they used to."

Nate nodded, taking that in. "You have a big house."

"Yes, I do." Lydia tweaked Nate's chin, eliciting a giggle. "And I'm very glad you're here to visit."

She looked up at Jameson then, and Nina could see tears pooling in the old woman's eyes. "Come say hello, Jameson."

He hesitated long enough to take Nina's hand and together they moved to his grandmother's side. "Hello, Lydia."

Leaning heavily on the walker, she took Jameson's hand. "It's so good to see you."

"I'm glad to see you, too."

Nina glanced up at Jameson and she saw only sincerity in his expression. She smiled at Lydia and offered her hand. "I'm Nina."

Lydia's grip was weak and trembling. "Thank you. For calling. For bringing Nate. And Jameson."

Nina could see the exhaustion lining Lydia's face. "Can we go in? It's been a long drive."

"Of course." Lydia motioned to her butler. "Devon, help me inside please."

"I can help, too," Nate announced. When Devon moved to Lydia's left, Nate took up a post on his great-grandmother's right side.

Jameson quickly crossed the portico to open the door. Once they were all inside, Devon helped Lydia into a motorized wheelchair waiting in the entryway. She sank into it gratefully.

"Would you bring us tea, Devon? We'll take it in the breakfast room."

Nate bent close to Lydia's ear and in a loud stage whisper, informed her, "I don't like tea, Great-grandma."

Lydia smiled. "Some milk as well. And don't forget the cookies."

When they reached the breakfast room, a sunny space with tall French doors providing a spectacular view of San Francisco Bay, Jameson took Nina's hand, pulling her close to his side. She glanced up at him, seeing clearly that he wanted her reassurance. He was a grown man with a power of his own, but in that moment he needed something only a woman could provide. She squeezed his hand and he put his arm around her.

Lydia didn't miss a beat, her shrewd blue eyes taking in their interaction even as she smiled at her great-grandson. "Take a look in the corner, Nate. I thought it would be fun to have a few things here for you."

Without further prompting, Nate went straight for the large, wooden toy chest and lifted the lid. It was packed with toys, some brand-new, some well-worn with play.

He pulled out an elaborate fire truck, one of the older toys. "Can I play with this?"

"Of course, pumpkin, that's why it's there," Lydia told him. "Take it out on the back patio if you like."

"Hold on, Nate," Jameson said. "Can I take a look at that?"

Nina saw a strange mix of emotions in Jameson's face as he took the fire truck from Nate. "Lydia, who's toy was this?"

Grief shone in Lydia's soft green eyes. "That was Sean's."

It shouldn't hurt so much. Jameson stared down at the toy in his hands, taking in how time and small fingers had aged it. The paper labels on the sides reading *Engine 22* were worn around the edges, and the extension on the ladder was missing. One of the firefighters seated in the front was missing an arm and the headlights had been colored black.

It shouldn't mean anything to him. He'd barely known his brother. He'd seen him just that one time when Sean was ten years old, during a trip to San Francisco just before he'd shipped out to Kuwait. Then several years later, Sean somehow tracked Jameson down and called him. In the midst of his wild, rebellious teens, Sean would phone Jameson late at night, loud and foulmouthed, sometimes high and angry at the world.

Then that one, ill-fated weekend with Sean in Sacramento. And now Sean's ashes sat in a box in the back of Jameson's closet.

Jameson returned the toy to Nate, then pushed open one of the French doors leading out to the patio. Nate smiled up at him and for a heart-wrenching moment, Jameson saw Sean's face overlaid on his son's. A punch in the gut would have been easier to ward off.

Nate skipped out onto the patio, then knelt on the

limestone tile and *vroomed* the fire engine in arcs around him. Volatile emotions ripped through Jameson, and he couldn't stand still. He stepped out on the patio, leaving the door open so Nina could keep an eye on Nate, then took off down the large, sloping lawn that led to a white gazebo. Just past the gazebo, a sandy trail meandered around his grandmother's estate, and he headed down the path.

If he could just outrun his feelings, his memories, his regrets. But he couldn't. He had to find a way to accept the consequences of his actions, his inactions, his decisions, good and bad. He had to find a way to put the pieces of his life back together.

You don't have to do it alone.

The realization froze him in his tracks. It wasn't just him anymore. He had Nina to buttress him, at least until they parted in two years time. Even then, she likely wouldn't be completely out of his life, not if he still maintained a connection with his son.

He stared out at the blue waters of San Francisco Bay. More than two months of those brief twenty-four had already passed. He was far from ready to let Nina go, couldn't imagine that another twenty-two months would accustom him to having her out of his life. His stomach churned at that inevitability.

He had to focus on the now while she was with him. He could lean on her, use her sweetness, her loving nature to support his weaknesses. Somehow he'd find a way to adjust to life without her.

With slow steps, he ascended the verdant green knoll again, his chest tightening when he caught sight of Nate playing with Sean's much-loved toy fire engine. He hadn't known his brother at age four, but maybe for a moment, he could watch Nate and imagine the kind of young boy Sean had been before he let the darkness swallow him.

Pulling up a wicker chair, Jameson sat near his son. As the afternoon sun sank toward the bay, he let himself pretend Nate's imaginative play was Sean's, let Nate open a window to a time he wished he had known, to a past forever lost.

When Jameson had first stalked off across the back lawn as if to escape some personal hell, Nina feared he might be gone for hours. But he'd barely gone out of eyesight before he returned to watch over Nate on the patio. Then when he returned inside, the uncharacteristic peace that had settled over him both surprised and pleased her.

While he still seemed to maintain an emotional distance from his grandmother, his obvious rancor for her seemed to have faded. When Lydia suggested they stay the night at her house instead of continuing into the city, Jameson surprised her again by graciously accepting the invitation. Later at dinner, which they ate in the kitchen because Lydia said she would feel ridiculous sitting at the massive dining room table when there were so few of them, Jameson helped her from her wheelchair into her chair, then back into the wheelchair afterward.

If Jameson's grandmother wondered at their request for separate rooms, she kept her conjecture to herself. Their excuse made perfect sense since Nate would be more comfortable sleeping with his mother in a strange house. But Lydia didn't voice an obvious alternative—

to bring a daybed for Nate into one of the villa's master suites, allowing Jameson and Nina to sleep together in the king-size bed.

Instead Nina slept on that wide bed with her son sprawled comalike on the other side. Or she would have slept if her skin wasn't prickling with jittery energy. She hadn't realized just how edgy she'd been, anticipating an explosion in Jameson that never came. Now that they'd all retreated to their respective corners, when she should finally be able to relax, she couldn't lie still.

Nina glanced at the clock. Just past midnight. They'd agreed to rise at seven to get an early start into the city. If she didn't find a way to soothe herself into sleep, she'd be a walking zombie in the morning.

When Nina eased from the bed, Nate didn't so much as stir. She dithered over whether to pull on her jeans and T-shirt, but decided the nightgown she wore was modest enough. In any case, everyone else was likely asleep. Devon, who lived over the garage, would only return to the house if alerted to a problem via the intercom between him and Lydia. Surely Nina wouldn't encounter anyone if she went down to the kitchen for some hot milk.

The soft creak of the bedroom door sounded loud in the quiet of the house. A quick check of Nate told her he still slumbered on, dead to the world. Padding along on bare feet along the carpet runner that ran the length of the hall, she moved soundlessly to the stairs.

It wasn't until she reached the first floor that she realized a light was on in the kitchen. The faint yellow glow illuminated the dining room as she passed through it. Assuming Devon had left the light on for Lydia in case she came down in the villa's elevator before he arrived in the morning, Nina expected the kitchen to be empty when she stepped inside.

She stopped short with a gasp when she spied Jameson across the kitchen. His head swung up and shadows sharpened the angles of his face in the pale light over the sink. He wore only his jeans and his broad shoulders were hunched as he stood leaning against the gleaming Sub-Zero refrigerator, a bottle of beer dangling from his fingers. His blue gaze locked with hers and burned with dark turbulence.

Whatever peace she'd sensed in him earlier had vanished, replaced by bleakness. He might have kept his devils at bay for a short while, but now she could see them nipping at his heels.

She urged her feet to move again until she stood a safe distance from him. "I couldn't sleep," she told him.

"Me, neither." He lifted the beer bottle and through the amber glass, Nina could see it was still full. "I thought this would help. Couldn't quite bring myself to drink it."

There was a weighty significance in his statement. Instead of asking straight out, she waited for him to continue on his own.

"I drank that night," he said finally. "One beer and part of a second."

A chill went through her as she realized what night he referred to. The night of the accident, a chain of events that sent him to prison. She knew only the Hart Valley busybodies' version of the events—that Jameson had been drunk, that someone had been killed. She hadn't wanted to think about the circumstances of that night, simply couldn't, and still marry him.

She almost walked out, not wanting to hear any more. But she could see the pain Jameson was in and knew she couldn't leave him.

So she stood before him, mesmerized by Jameson's story. "The change in Sean shocked me. Not just because he was older. But because he looked so…ruined."

Jameson set the beer aside on the kitchen island, next to the cook top. Head tipped down, he crossed his arms over his chest. His biceps flexed tautly as if he tried to hold the memories back in.

"He was completely wasted by the time I found him at the bar. I don't know what he'd had before he started drinking. The four or five beers he downed finished him off."

Nina wanted to reach out, to touch him. Or slap on the overhead lights, the bright fluorescents that might drive away the shadows in the corners. That would break the spell, stop the words spilling from the tortured man who stood before her. She forced herself to keep still.

"I couldn't let him drive. I knew that." The harshness in Jameson's voice scraped along Nina's nerves. "I had to take away his keys. No matter what, I couldn't let him behind the wheel."

As if the horror of that night had overtaken him, blotted out his will, he shut his eyes, covered his face with his hands. "The crash seemed so unreal. Lasting an eternity, over in an instant."

He dropped his hands and they shook spastically. "I thought I saw her face. They told me I couldn't have because of the glare. I saw her afterwards, and the…" He swallowed convulsively. "The little girl."

He lifted his gaze to Nina. "There was no damn way I wouldn't take responsibility. The lawyer wanted me to change my story, do some legal tap-dance, but I wouldn't. Couldn't. I had to be the one to stand up, because Sean…"

Nina thought she understood. Sean had to see that a man faced up to the consequences of his actions, as horrible as his actions might have been. "Did it help?" she asked gently. "Seeing you take responsibility—did he get clean, off the drugs?"

Almost as if he had forgotten she was there, Jameson stared uncomprehendingly for a moment before the sense of her question sank in. He shook his head, the grief in his eyes unbearable. "No. The drugs finally killed him." His chest heaved as he gripped his hands into fists. "My sacrifice meant nothing."

My sacrifice. He'd pleaded guilty to a crime he'd committed…how was that a sacrifice? Because he'd faced up to his actions as a lesson to his brother, rather than take the easy out the attorney had offered? But somehow she knew Jameson wouldn't have taken the easy way in any case. If he was responsible, he would have pled guilty.

My sacrifice. She had to know what he'd meant. Had to ask.

She barely had time to open her mouth, take a breath. In the next moment, he'd closed the distance between them, pulled her into his arms. The hot bare skin of his chest felt like heaven pressed against her, his hands stroking the length of her back through the thin knit of her nightgown, like paradise. Then his mouth on hers redefined ecstasy.

Chapter Eleven

He'd kept the story locked inside himself for so long. He'd barely allowed himself to think about that night, let alone speak of it since the day he'd given testimony in a sealed courtroom. His only witnesses had been the judge, the attorneys, the court reporter…and the husband and older son of the woman killed. All those long nights in prison, he would see their eyes, their grief, their pain.

He forced his focus back to Nina, her soft lips caressing his, the taste of her as his tongue thrust inside her mouth. Holding Nina in his arms, he could burn away the old, dark memories, let the agony of the past tumble into blackness. The ardor of Nina's kiss had the power to vanquish the gravest transgression.

He felt her hands against his chest, felt the imprint of each finger. Imagined those hands stroking him down his chest, along his belly, diving beneath the waistband of his jeans. The heavy throb of heat low in his body stole his breath. He moved closer, pressed against the yielding vee of her legs.

Her quiet cry sifted into his ears, and he tipped her head back to get better access to her mouth. His hand drifted down her body, along her throat, across her shoulder, to the tender mound of her breast. When he drew his palm across her nipple, her low urgent moan shot through him, and his hips thrust toward her without conscious volition.

He didn't care in that moment that they stood in his grandmother's kitchen, that they could be discovered if the butler happened to see the light and come over to investigate. All he wanted was to be inside Nina, to feel her welcome him, take him over the edge, beyond the horrors he could never seem to leave behind.

Even when he felt the pressure of her hands against his chest increase, he didn't relent at first. But she grew more insistent until he couldn't deny her silent request. He loosened his hold and she drew back, her eyes wide, her mouth moist and tempting.

Letting her go gave him the chance to think, and he was desperate for the oblivion of sensation. But although he tried to urge her closer, she resisted, implacable. She didn't say a word, just shook her head.

He backed away, feeling like a damn coward, needing her so much. But he'd told her nearly everything, all but the most tightly held secret, and he felt as vulnerable and stripped bare as a man flayed.

"Don't run," she said gently. "Please."

He looked over at her, stunned. In another moment, he would have been out the door, down that ocean path, escaping. She'd realized it before he had.

She moved nearer, put out her hand. "Jameson—"

"Don't." He raised his hand to ward her off. At her wounded look he forced a smile. "Right now, if you touch me…" He heaved in a breath. "I don't think I could let you go again."

If he wondered whether her response was any less than his, it was answered by the way her gaze strayed from his face, down his body, to where his hard flesh pressed against the placket of his jeans. The heat in her dark brown eyes when she lifted her gaze to his made it nearly impossible to steel himself against the desire to pull her toward him.

She stepped back to lean against the kitchen island, her arms wrapped around herself. "You need to find a way to forgive yourself."

That was the last thing he'd expected her to say. "I can't. And I shouldn't."

"Why not?"

"You shouldn't even have to ask." He felt suddenly restless and he paced away from her to stare out at the dark garden outside the kitchen window. "It was an unforgivable act. They're dead because of me." There was another layer to that truth, one known to only a handful of living people—his grandmother, his lawyer, the judge who signed his release papers.

"It was an accident."

"Caused by irresponsibility."

He looked back at her, saw the resignation in her face. In a flash of insight, Jameson realized Nina had been looking for a way to forgive him, to rationalize away the wrongness of what had been done that night. But not even Nina, the most giving and charitable of women, could do it. She couldn't bring herself to excuse his sins.

Unless she knew the whole truth. What had really happened. With one simple admission, he could wipe away all her mistrust, the pain of acknowledging that the man she'd married had done the unthinkable. He would have to offer up Sean's soul, blot out any vestige of light that might be lingering over that box of ashes in his closet. What would it matter, with Sean dead?

Yet it seemed the most cowardly act of all. When Sean wasn't here, couldn't explain for himself his tortured life, the abyss of fear and anger in which he'd lived. If there was nothing else Jameson could do for his brother, he would protect that last flickering flame that had once been Sean. If it was not done in memory of a good man, then in recognition of what could have been.

"I can't change it, Nina. And I can't bring them back. What's the point of forgiving myself?"

The sadness in her face grabbed at his throat, and he was shocked to feel the threat of tears. He hadn't cried under the worst of his father's beatings, had stood stone-faced at his mother's funeral. But Nina's empathy was nearly his undoing.

"Have to get back to bed," he said, turning away. "We have an early morning."

He didn't let himself stop until he'd retraced his path through the house, then upstairs and into his bedroom. He shut the door quietly behind him, leaned against it as if it needed buttressing against his pursuing demons. Taking silent breaths as he waited for Nina's footfalls up the stairs, he listened as she moved along the landing, inside her and Nate's room. Once he heard the sound of her latch closing, he let himself sink to the floor, aching to the core, awash in agony.

Nina sat with Lydia and Nate at the kitchen table, sunlight spilling into the windows overlooking the back lawn. Nate leaned back in his chair in a state of sugar-induced bliss after inhaling a huge stack of Devon's pancakes. Nina had picked at her own flapjacks despite their fluffy, golden-brown perfection. Lydia had daintily eaten one, and now sat with her coffee cup cradled in her hands, her gaze on Nina.

The breakfast conversation had been pleasant, barely scratching beneath the surface. Lydia had asked about the café and they'd discussed the foibles of running one's own business. She was curious about Hart Valley, the small foothills town her daughter, Julia, had spent her last years living in, and seemed hungry for details. Nina had wished she'd had more to tell Lydia about Jameson's mother.

It was nearly eight, and Jameson still hadn't made an appearance. Nina briefly wondered if he'd made one of his great escapes, running away from the tortured emotions that haunted him. But when she'd stepped out onto the front portico early this morning to watch the sunrise, she saw the Camry still parked below.

Nina reached for the French coffee press and topped off her cup. She'd have to wake Jameson soon if they wanted to get into the city. The trade show opened at nine and she'd hoped to arrive early enough to avoid some of the crowds. As it was, they'd be fighting traffic getting to the Moscone Center.

At the sink, Devon finished washing the skillet and

mixing bowls and put the last of the dishes in the dishwasher. He turned to Lydia expectantly.

She smiled at her great-grandson. "Nate, Devon needs some help pruning roses in the garden. Would you mind giving him a hand?"

Lydia's thinly veiled request to baby-sit seemed to be no surprise to Devon. His angular face remained impassive as he coaxed Nate from the table with the promise of outfitting him with his own garden gloves and shears. They left the kitchen hand in hand.

Lydia sat back in her chair, the light from the windows softening the lines of her face. "Devon's duties go beyond those of an ordinary man-servant. He worked several years as a paramedic, cared for his wife through the final stages of ovarian cancer. He lost his wife, lost his job, lost his house. I needed full-time care and he was a godsend."

Lydia hadn't sent Nate out of the room to discuss her butler. Nina waited out the silence that ensued, the long moments while Lydia lifted her coffee cup and sipped from it, set it down. A trace of color rose in the old woman's cheeks.

Finally, the words were wrung out of her. "I can't forget his face. The grief. The fear. The hopelessness."

"Whose face?" Nina knew, but she wanted the admission in the open.

"Jameson's." She gripped her hands together on the table, staring down at them. "I deserve the worst hell has to offer for leaving that little boy behind."

Nina couldn't hold back the edge of anger in her voice. "Didn't you know the kind of man you were leaving him with?"

"I suspected." She lifted her gaze to Nina. "Julia would call when she knew Garret was out of the house and we'd talk. But all those years of seeing how her father treated me, perhaps she thought that was the only way men could be."

"Then your husband hit you, too?"

Bitterness darkened Lydia's face. "He didn't have to. He knew other ways to terrify and humiliate." She shook her head. "That doesn't justify my cowardice. Nothing Garret could have done to me would have been worse than what Jameson suffered."

Lydia's misery tugged at Nina's heart. Moving her chair closer, she put her hand over the older woman's. "You have to go forward from here. You have a chance at a new start with Jameson."

She sighed, and a certain peace seemed to blanket her. They sat in silence for several moments, then Lydia smiled. "And what about you, my dear? What kind of start have you made with my grandson?"

The sudden change of topic threw Nina off-guard. "I don't know what you mean."

"This marriage of yours can't have been a love match." Lydia's gaze sharpened shrewdly. "At least not at the outset."

Nina didn't like the implication in Lydia's statement. "We respect each other."

Lydia's unladylike snort demonstrated what she thought of Nina's pallid assertion. "There was obviously something between you before Jameson went to prison. Nate is the proof of that. But you never visited him at Folsom. I would have known. So whatever your relationship is now has developed since his release."

"We don't have a relationship," Nina protested.

Lydia laughed out loud. "You might not have intended to have one. I can imagine how this marriage came about. My grandson discovered he had a son and insisted he marry you. You objected, but Jameson managed to convince you."

Annoyance flickered inside Nina at the old woman's savvy. "You seem to have it all figured out."

Lydia patted Nina's arm with a gnarled hand. "But have you, my dear?"

As Lydia's provocative query dangled in the air, the sound of footsteps turned Nina away from the older woman's probing gaze. She expected to see Devon and Nate in the kitchen doorway. Instead, Jameson stood there, dark hair still damp from a shower, a T-shirt tucked into black denims that shaped his narrow hips temptingly. Nina had to school herself to stay in her chair instead of rising to cross the room, to put her arms around him.

She quickly scanned his face, but saw no trace of last night's anguish. He seemed to have sealed those emotions off, walled them away. Maybe he thought that if he ignored them, they'd simply vanish.

Nina wished her own feelings would vanish as well. Wished that Lydia had never asked that question. Because seeing Jameson now in his grandmother's sun-kissed kitchen, the answer screamed at her. Even her own very logical mind suggested that her feelings had perhaps transformed into something much stronger.

Two years. That was all she'd committed to. Within that short span of time, she could allow herself a certain fondness for Jameson, respect for him. But there was no room in their temporary marriage for anything more. She simply wouldn't allow it.

With his first glimpse of Nina, Jameson could barely take a breath. Her vivid red V-neck, her sleek black hair tucked behind one ear revealing an onyx earring, her brown eyes glowing with a light that gripped his heart—in that moment, his emotions were completely out of control.

As he stepped inside the kitchen, he turned his focus on his grandmother. "Good morning, Lydia." The yearning in his grandmother's face compelled him to give her a kiss on the cheek. Her smile loosened some of the tension in him.

"Good morning, Grandson."

He desperately wanted to touch Nina, gather her in his arms and carry her off to that wide king-size bed he'd slept alone in last night. Instead he brushed her shoulder lightly with his fingertips. "We should go."

Nina pushed back her chair and rose quickly. "I'll find Nate."

"I have an idea," Lydia said, climbing to her feet more slowly. "Why not leave Nate with me for the day? I'm sure he'd be bored silly with the trade show."

Nina glanced over at him, her expression wary. "We have a reservation in the city. We'd planned to spend the night, then head home in the morning."

His grandmother's smile broadened. "Then leave him here overnight. You two can pick him up on your way home tomorrow. I'd love the chance for some one-on-one time with my great-grandson. Devon will be here to give me a hand with him."

A day and a night alone with Nina. As much as he loved his son, cherished their time together, solitary moments with Nina were even more precious. To have a day together, just the two of them—they could take their time at the trade show, go out to dinner, maybe see a film. Then spend the night together....

He shook off that possibility, unwilling to stray into dangerous territory. "We'd have to ask Nate."

At that moment, Nate returned with Devon in tow. "Mommy, they got a little house made of windows and they got strawberries growing in there. Devon let me eat some." He rubbed his belly to show how good they were.

The prospect of staying the night at his great-grandmother's thrilled Nate. Jumping up and down, he bounced around the kitchen hollering at the top of his lungs.

Nina watched their son with a bemused smile. "I thought he might be a little more concerned at being left behind."

His grandmother shuffled sideways toward her walker, waving off Jameson's move to help her. "You've obviously raised him to be independent and self-sufficient. That's a good thing."

With Devon's assistance, Lydia took Nate out to the back patio while Jameson and Nina gathered up their things. Jameson couldn't allow himself to think as he carried their luggage down to the Camry. His body was roaring with awareness, at a fever pitch in anticipation of undivided time with Nina.

They returned to the portico to say their goodbyes. Nate gave them both enthusiastic hugs and noisy kisses before dragging Devon back into the house. Nina put her arms gently around Jameson's frail grandmother before heading down to the car to wait for him.

Her hands gripped the walker so tightly, her knuckles were white with strain. "I'm so sorry," she whispered.

Her earnest apology shifted something inside him, loosened a jagged piece of anger he'd held on to for so long. He realized suddenly he could let that go, could forgive.

"I'm sorry, too," he told her. "That I couldn't... change things with Sean."

She gave him a stern look. "He wasn't your responsibility. It's time to stop taking the blame."

That he couldn't agree with, but he held his tongue. "Thanks for taking care of Nate."

Her impish smile mirrored Nate's mischievous grin. "I'm glad to give you two newlyweds time alone."

The reminder brought the heat back to his body. After a peck on the cheek from his grandmother, Jameson descended the stairs. It was nearly nine o'clock, much later than they had planned to depart for the city. But without Nate, they'd be able to make their way through the trade show floor more efficiently, so the lost time wouldn't be an issue.

As he wended his way through his grandmother's exclusive neighborhood then pulled onto Interstate 280, a question burned in the back of his mind. He waited until he'd merged into freeway traffic before he voiced it. "Should we keep the two rooms?"

She didn't pretend ignorance of the implication of her answer. Her hands locked in her lap, head bowed, he could sense the sizzle of heat inside her that echoed to his own. If she said yes, that she still wanted her own room, it would drive him crazy with pent-up lust. But he'd accept her decision. He'd take as many cold showers as necessary to try to wash away the desire. If that was even possible.

She cleared her throat, glancing over at him. When she shook her head and said softly, "No," he veered over the warning bumps, earning the angry honk of an SUV before he returned safely to his own lane.

Tonight they'd be sharing a room. They'd be sharing a bed. He doubted he'd be able to think of anything else until then.

Then she reached over and brushed the back of her fingers against his cheek. The gesture was so tender, her gaze so caring, that joy rocketed through him, erasing thought, erasing even desire, and leaving in its wake an unfathomable emotion.

As they strolled through the Esplanade Ballroom at San Francisco's Moscone Center, Jameson stayed at Nina's side, overwhelming her, oversensitizing her to everything around her. The soft roar of the crowd squeezing past her as they moved from exhibit to exhibit, the delectable smells of food samples offered, the dizzying variety of cookware, restaurant equipment and supplies were all magnified by the constant touch of Jameson's hand. It was both an exhilaration experiencing it all with him, and torture anticipating the scintillating temptation that waited for them that evening.

She would have thought nothing could match their night of white lightning five years ago. It had been impulsive and unexpected, both of them pushed over the edge before they could even think. She'd felt dazed in the aftermath, too mind-blown even for regret.

But spontaneity had nothing on the feelings slowly building inside her today. They'd been holding passion at bay for weeks now. Even when they'd succumbed, they'd pulled back before consummation, only stoking the pending conflagration to even greater potential.

She'd spent five years denying that their one-night stand might have been something more than just an encounter between two lusty bodies. She'd insisted to herself that her longing for an unattainable man had left her vulnerable to Jameson, to his passion.

It had taken only opportunity—a marriage, a shared life—to explode that myth. Jameson's secrets, the hidden layers of himself he was loath to reveal, only prodded her to want to know him better. Watching him interact with their son, reveling in his solicitousness toward her, had stealthily built something atop the foundation they'd laid years earlier. If she loved him now, it was only because she'd begun to love him then.

As they moved through the packed exhibit hall, her heart seemed to open to him with each moment, expand with each touch, each smile. He seemed as interested as she was in even the most mundane items on display, and demonstrated that he understood the tools, supplies and equipment needed for the restaurant trade almost better than she did. That he'd made the effort to learn about something that was so much a part of her life pleased her, warmed her inside.

Now, his arm around her shoulders, he guided her through the crowd, a man on a mission. He referred quickly to the vendor guide, then changed course, heading for a particularly thick knot of people around a display of stove-top cookware.

He urged her to the front of the crowd to the display of stainless steel cookware. A sixty-quart stockpot held front and center among the other, smaller items arranged around it.

Jameson gestured at the stockpot. "This is the size you've been looking for."

"I have other pots."

"Nothing this big," he reminded her. "You could make bigger batches of soup weekly and freeze it, instead of having to make it every day."

She checked the price tag and winced. "I hate to spend the money."

"Then don't. Let me buy it." He reached for his wallet.

"Wait—" She put her hand out to stop him before he could pass his credit card to the woman behind the display. "You can't keep spending your money on me."

"Of course I can." He pulled out of her grasp and gave the woman his card. "Can I get this shipped?"

The warm glow of a few minutes earlier faded at his obstinacy. "You're paying the mortgage, for most of the food at home. You buy Nate every little thing he asks for."

He quickly signed the credit slip. "Don't worry about it."

"I do worry. There can't be much left from what you made doing construction work."

Scribbling out the address for the café, he put his arm around Nina again and ducked through the crowd. "Are you ready for lunch?"

She shrugged off his arm and faced him. "Talk to me,

Jameson. Where is the money coming from? I don't want you going into debt."

He laughed, but there was no humor in the sound. "There's no danger of that."

Taking his hand in hers, she shook it gently. "Then tell me. What is this endless source of money?"

For a moment he wouldn't meet her gaze. Then he put his arm around her. "Let's take a walk."

With Jameson holding her close to his side, they made their way out of the convention center and onto Fourth Street. The December chill seemed to muffle the sounds of the city, the slate-gray skies glowering over them. At first they kept their conversation on the surface, engaging in small talk, dancing around the unspoken topic with commentary about the trade show. Jameson had left his jacket in the car, but his body generated enough heat to warm Nina despite her thin sweater.

They crossed busy Market Street, ambling on until they reached Union Square. They wandered around the square, Christmas decorations glittering in the shop windows.

"It's my grandmother's money," Jameson finally said. "A trust."

"I don't understand why you'd want to keep that secret."

"I didn't want it." He bit out the words. "Never wanted it."

Nina stayed quiet, waited for him to continue. They'd made a complete circuit of the square and now he urged her toward one of the concrete ledges along Geary Street. They sat alongside tourists, shoppers, other trade show attendees looking for a respite from the crowd.

Her hand on his lap, he idly stroked the back of it with his palm. The sensual awareness that had ebbed now returned, full-force.

"The money was my mother's originally," he said quietly, his gaze on their linked hands. "To be given to her at age thirty. She was twenty-six when she died."

A police siren blared nearby. Jameson waited until it had passed. "When my grandparents took custody of Sean, they transferred the trust to him. Then when he died…"

Breaking the connection between them, he leaned forward, elbows on his knees, head bowed. "It seems so wrong. Sean's money paid my way out of prison, bought the house. It'll put Nate through college some day. I shouldn't be spending it, should give it back—"

"Why? Your grandmother obviously wants you to have it."

"It's not mine. I didn't work for it. I did nothing to deserve it. Lydia's trying to soothe her guilt with it, but she's got to know that no amount of money will do that."

"Guilt—for leaving you with your father?"

"She's letting that go." He looked back at her. "We both are. Because we can change it now. But some things can't ever be rectified."

Nina took a breath. "The woman who died." Jameson nodded. "But why would your grandmother feel guilt at that? When she wasn't at all involved?"

Jameson grew still, his gaze locked with hers. Something flickered in his eyes, an awareness that he'd said too much. Then he looked away again. "I don't know."

But he did. Nina was certain of that. What she didn't know was why he wouldn't tell her, why he still kept so much bottled up inside.

He stretched his hand out to her. "I want to check in at the hotel."

As she took his hand, sensation shot up her spine, seared along her nerve endings. All her anticipation kicked into overdrive, set her heart to thundering in her ears.

In that moment, she couldn't think of the past anymore, or Jameson's secrets. The only mysteries she cared about was how his mouth would feel against hers, his hand stroking her skin, his fingers exploring her most intimate places.

The past could resolve itself later. Now she wanted to be close to Jameson.

Chapter Twelve

When they'd arrived in the city, they'd left their car in the hotel parking structure and walked to the Moscone Center. Now as they returned to the hotel, with Nina's heart galloping at breakneck speed, their pace seemed maddeningly slow. Nina felt ready to implode from pent-up frustration in the few short blocks back to Fifth Street.

She hung back with their luggage in the opulent lobby as Jameson checked in, impatient when he had to wait behind several dark-suited businessmen. When he finally rejoined her with the card key, he looked so serious, she couldn't resist sharing a sudden crazy notion.

"Did you check us in as Mr. and Mrs. Smith?" she asked breathlessly.

His surprise gave way to a devastating smile so incredibly sexy, she was half-tempted to start undressing him in the lobby. He bent and pressed a kiss to her brow, a sweet gesture that somehow seemed hotter than the most intimate of touches. She was glad for the support of his arm as they made their way to the elevator; she wasn't sure she could keep to her feet otherwise.

They had the elevator car to themselves up to the fifth floor and Jameson put those few moments alone to good use, pressing her against the wall, burning her up with his kiss. His hand slipped under her sweater, his fingertips grazing her bare skin when the bell dinged for their floor.

They found their room, and Jameson fumbled with the key card a moment before he could release the lock. They made it inside, tossed aside their bags. Tight in each other's arms, they kissed as they edged across the room to the bed. They tumbled down, still fully dressed, Jameson on top of her.

After a long, drugging kiss, he pulled back and flashed that seldom seen, but oh-so-sexy smile. "This is nearly how we did it before. More clothes on than off."

Her hands cradling his head, she returned his smile. "We're older now. More mature. Maybe we could take it slower this time."

He lowered his head and nuzzled her ear, pulling a groan from her. "I want to see you naked. I want to see every part of you."

He eased himself from the bed and kicked off his shoes, pulled off his shirt. When he bent toward her again, she whispered, "Wait."

Rising, she slipped her own shoes off, then laid her hands against his skin. He sucked in a breath, his hands gripping her shoulders. "That feels too damn good."

She moved her hands, stroking across his hot skin, feeling the ridges of his taut belly, the striation of muscles along his sides, the angles of his collarbone and shoulders. If there was such a thing as a perfect man, Jameson was it.

Her gaze fell to the ripple of a scar on his left side. She ran her hand down over it and he shuddered. "How did you get this?"

"At Folsom," he gasped out as she trailed her fingers over it again. "Man with a knife. Out in the yard."

She wished she could erase that scar and the horrifying memories it represented. That magic was beyond her, but maybe her touch would help him forget. Her restless hands wandered to the thin line of dark hair that led down into his black denims. His fingers tightened on her shoulders as she traced along the waistband of his jeans. When she reached for the button of his fly, his hand on hers stopped her.

"Wait," he said hoarsely. "Slower, remember?"

Nudging her hands aside, he took the hem of her sweater and peeled it off her before tossing it away. His gaze riveted on her breasts, so avid, so rapt, she was grateful their generous size gave him pleasure. Then he touched her, featherlight, along the lace cups of her bra and she thought she would melt.

"Men tell women they have beautiful eyes," he said with a trace of humor in his tone. "You do." Fingertips under her bra straps, he pushed them off her shoulders. "But I have to admit to a certain fascination with your breasts."

He reached behind to unhook her bra and let it fall away. His hands grazed so lightly over her breasts, she thought she'd go insane. She wanted his hands molded to her soft flesh, wanted him to cup them, kiss them.

He sensed her urgency, whispered, "Slower..."

Turning to sit at the edge of the bed, he tugged her between his legs and buried his face in the valley between her breasts. Hands cradling them on either side, he trailed his tongue along the tender underside of each one. He flicked at her nipple with the tip of his tongue as he passed—too much sensation, not nearly enough.

She moaned, awareness exploding in all directions. His hands drifted down to her jeans, releasing the button and zipper, he eased them off her hips. He let her step out of them, returning his attentions to her breasts. She felt a faint disappointment that he hadn't removed her panties, too. Then he drew her nipple into his mouth and she cried out with the exquisite pleasure.

He drew back, his mouth meandering to her other breast. "I can't wait to see you climax." As he teased her other nipple, she felt warmth between her legs. *Slower. Slower.*

Too restless to stand still any longer, she decided turnabout was fair play. With a gentle push, she guided Jameson back up onto the bed. Straddling his hips, she let her breasts brush across his bare chest as she leaned down to kiss him.

She lowered her hips just enough to press the vee of her legs against the bulge straining at the placket of his jeans. A long, low groan vibrated through his body and Nina felt a sense of triumph at the sound. When the urgency rose to strip off her panties, to take him into her body, she put it aside, drawing more pleasure from the enforced delay.

"Slower," she murmured against his mouth.

His hands moved along her sides, wrists grazing the

sides of her breasts, palms nipping in at her waist. He paused at the waistband of her panties, then hooked his thumbs in and leisurely drew them down. She shifted away to let him pull them free, then stretched out beside him.

Following his lead, she took her time unbuttoning and unzipping, taking off the black denims, then his shorts with slow strokes of her hands. She wanted to touch his thrusting flesh immediately, cup the softness below. But she forced herself to enjoy the feel of his legs, rough with dark hair, his smooth hips.

At a sudden realization, her touch faltered. He covered her hand with his. "What?"

She met his gaze, his eyes nearly black with desire. "I don't have protection."

"I do." He pulled away, grabbed his jeans from the floor and fished out a small square packet. He set it aside on the nightstand.

He lay beside her again, feathered soft kisses across her mouth, along her jaw. A flick of his tongue in the whorls of her ear, teeth on the tender lobe scraping gently. Pushing her onto her back, his mouth moved lower along her throat to her collarbone, down to the first soft swell of her breast.

She explored his body in return, fingertips light along the ridge of his spine, tracing the striations of his back where muscles lay taut under his heated flesh. When he raised himself up to look down at her, his face hot with passion, she spanned his broad chest with her hands, moving them restlessly from shoulders to tight belly.

Then his clever fingers moved along her ribcage, past the dip of her waist, below the rounded curve of her hip. His hand grazed the curls of hair at the apex of her legs. He teased that way, the barest touch, over and over, until her heart thundered in her ears. Then he wove his fingers into the soft hair, traced the seam with slow, nerve-searing patience. When her legs parted of their own accord, he dipped inside oh so slightly, just enough to have her nearly screaming with sensation.

She wanted to touch him the same way, teasing, torturing, but he'd pressed himself against her hip out of reach. The length of him, hard and ready, burned her, left her yearning for fulfillment. She thrust against him, heard him gasp. He groaned deep in his chest.

Pressing another kiss between her breasts, he reached for the foil packet on the nightstand. Once he'd sheathed himself, he settled his hips between her legs. His upper body supported by his arms, he gazed down at her, his expression serious and dark with passion. "Yes?" he asked.

Even so close to the edge, he left the final choice to her. "Yes," she whispered in return.

With his first thrust inside her, her eyes drifted shut, the clamoring sensations overwhelming. It felt tight, but her body adjusted, despite the years since she'd last made love.

His voice strained, he asked, "Okay?"

She opened her eyes and smiled up at him. "Way beyond okay." Her hands stroked down his sides to his hips, inviting him to move.

Tension marked his face, tightened the muscles of his arms, caught his breath each time he dragged in air. His tension fed her own, urgency and need warring with the desire to prolong the pleasure. She wanted his strokes inside her body to be slow, to last forever. She wanted them fast, to race them both to completion.

Before long, their bodies took over, deciding the rhythm. She stopped thinking, could only feel as the rapture grew, expanded within her. Frenzied passion ruled her body, wiped away coherent thought. At the same time, her heart seemed to grow a hundred times in size, filling with joy, a powerful connection with the man in her arms.

She cried out as climax hit, bursting in a million brilliant sparks. She heard Jameson's answering triumph as he followed her into ecstasy. Pulling him close, she gasped as a second wave hit her, bathed her in ardent delight.

His face buried in her neck, he made to shift his weight from her. She held on tighter. "Stay. You feel so good."

He levered only slightly off her, every inch of him still in contact with her. "I should clean up," he murmured against her throat.

"One more minute." She nuzzled the side of his face, enjoying the faint rasp of his beard against her cheek.

Finally she let him go and he disappeared for a few moments into the bathroom. When he returned, he stretched out beside her and after pulling the bedspread over them, gathered her in his arms. Nina shifted to her side, and Jameson lay on his back, gazing out into the dim room.

In the aftermath of their exquisite lovemaking, reason returned. When she'd agreed to a short-term marriage, it had been the only way she could accept the impossible situation of marrying a virtual stranger.

But he wasn't a stranger to her anymore. He'd become important to her, integral not only to her life, but to Nate's. And she'd allowed herself to become intimate with him, tearing down a vital barrier she'd kept between him and her heart.

She remembered that surge of joy she'd felt just before climax took her. That joy still infused her, coalescing into one clear, inescapable emotion. Love.

She squeezed her eyes shut in a panic, suddenly afraid Jameson would see what must be plainly written on her face. She waited, listening to his breathing, anticipating his questions. If he asked her flat out, she wouldn't be able to lie. And she was scared to death to admit the truth.

When his breathing slowed, deepened, she chanced a quick glance. He'd drifted off to sleep, the lines of his face relaxed. A peace had settled over him, not just from his body's repose, but as if from something deeper inside him that had finally moved toward acceptance. She'd never seen him sleep, but she sensed this was a profound change in him.

If she told him she loved him, would it enhance that peace, or shatter it? Would he let himself be loved? Would he ever feel the same way about her?

Her well-being faded, replaced by a gnawing anxiety. She wasn't ready to love him. So much still lay unresolved between them. Jameson's heart was still a fortress, guarding places inside himself that he might never allow her into. She could pound and pound away at that stone and never so much as crack the facade.

Could she accept that? Could she feel complete giving her love endlessly with no expectation that he'd return it? In that moment, she didn't have an answer.

Suddenly tears clogged her throat, their grip so tight she could barely breathe. Before she'd realized what she was doing, she was out of bed, on her feet. She hurried soundlessly to the bathroom, shutting the door as quietly as she could.

The fluorescent light showed her a stranger in the mirror. Her wild hair tumbled around her face, her lips still swollen with Jameson's lovemaking. A flush still colored her cheeks and her tender breasts. Despite her confusion, the tears burning her eyes, she wanted nothing more than to return to the bed, wake Jameson, start all over.

Gripping the edge of the tile countertop, she closed her eyes and took in a breath, trying to puzzle out what had driven her from the bed. She should have felt safe there, secure. Jameson was her husband; he should be her protection, her rock.

When it hit her, she hunched over the bathroom sink, aching as a fist of pain struck her middle. Memories rushed in—five years ago, lying in Jameson's arms, the nascent spark of joy she'd felt. She recognized now the potential to love him that existed even then. If he'd stayed with her, hadn't gone to Sacramento that weekend, hadn't been in that car with his brother, the seed of love could have bloomed between them. There would still be Nate, but instead of years without his father, Nate would have grown up knowing Jameson.

But he didn't stay. He'd set events in motion that tore him away from her. He might not have ever intended to leave her alone and pregnant with his child, but he'd done it nonetheless. And the pain of that abandonment that she'd never acknowledged swelled up inside her, an endless well of hurt she'd kept suppressed all these years.

The grief of it slammed into her. So much lost time. Irreplaceable moments of Nate's life—first tears, first smile, first words. His toddler years when he was everywhere and into everything all at once. Then later, as his face formed into a mirror image of his father's, so much goodness and wonder, gone forever. Jameson could never have it back.

Sobs shook her, quiet and desperate. The litany rolled over and over in her head—why did he go, why did he go? He'd abandoned so much. Not just her, but a piece of his own life he could never reclaim.

But he was here now. They could go forward from here.

Only a short time ago, the two years she'd promised him had seemed too long. Now it seemed far too limited. So why not tell him she'd reconsidered, that she wanted the marriage to be permanent? He'd wanted that in the first place; he'd be glad to extend their time together. Wouldn't her love for him be enough to sustain a marriage?

But one last misgiving lodged inside her, blocking her heart. Jameson's past—his part in the deaths of a mother and her child—hung far more heavily over her than she cared to admit. He'd admitted his guilt, done his time in prison. She knew intellectually there was no changing what had happened. Still, the reality of that act lingered like a ghost at the edge of her consciousness.

To confess her love to Jameson without completely coming to terms with what he'd done would be dishonest, would cheat them both. Until she could accept Jameson's past, could give her love freely without expectations, she would keep her love concealed.

She bent to the sink and splashed handfuls of water on her face. When she confirmed that all traces of her tears had been washed away, she returned to the room. Jameson still slept, the peace she'd seen before still softening his features, relaxing the angles and planes of his body. As much as she envied him his peace, she knew it would vanish with the first moments of wakefulness. That, more than anything, kept her from lying beside him again, waking him to invite another round of lovemaking.

Instead, she found her clothes and dressed, then pulled a book from her bag and sat beside the window to read. Emotions still rampaged through her—intense love for Jameson that seemed to grow by the moment, fear of abandonment that still clung with sharp claws, aching confusion. The cozy mystery did nothing to hold the miasma at bay, in fact she couldn't remember a word she read. An hour later, when the last of the afternoon light barely illuminated the page, she gave up the pretense of any interest in the book in her hand. There was far more mystery in watching Jameson sleep.

The instant he awoke Jameson knew she wasn't beside him. He sat bolt upright, searching for her first with his hands, then his eyes. But the bed was empty and the room so dark he could barely get his bearings, let alone discern what was furniture and what might be Nina. Reaching for the bedside light, he snapped it on and found her, leaning awkwardly in one of the chairs by the window, sound asleep.

Even if he hadn't had to wake her to save her from a stiff neck, he would have simply because he needed her close to him. Their lovemaking this afternoon had been light-years beyond what he'd experienced five years ago when they'd conceived Nate. As mind-blowing as he'd thought that had been, he had no real concept of paradise until now.

He wanted more of it. He wanted to keep Nina in this room for days, weeks, sampling, tasting every part of her, inventing new ways to give pleasure. He wanted to hear her moan again, hear her scream his name as he brought her to climax. He wanted her to collapse in his arms, too sated and satisfied to ever leave him. Then he'd start all over again.

Impossible, of course. Nate was waiting for them at his grandmother's, and as much as he wanted to ravage Nina, he very much wanted to be with his son again. He and Nina and Nate were a family, and that filled him, completed him as much as his lovemaking with his wife had.

Rising from the bed, he crossed the room and brushed a hand across Nina's cheek. She stirred, sighing as she awoke, making a face as she straightened her neck. When she became aware of him, her expression grew wary.

Anxiety twinged within him. He ignored it, smiling down at her. "I couldn't let you sleep like that."

She stretched, wriggling her shoulders. Her breasts pressed against the soft red knit, a seductive enticement. His flesh filled and her gaze dropped to his arousal. The sound of her gasp raced along his nerves, making him even harder.

Something enigmatic flickered in her face, and he would have given a dozen years of his life to know what ran through her mind. Then she stood, a smile curving her lush mouth, and slowly pulled off her sweater.

Wrapping her arms around him, she pressed herself against him, driving the breath from his lungs and reason from his brain.

Slowly was never a consideration from the moment they hit the bed. He had the rest of her clothes off in seconds, was grabbing for a condom and sheathing himself moments later. With his first thrust inside her, she screamed his name, a fantasy made flesh. Her climax rolled over her so quickly he hadn't a chance of holding back his own. After their deliberate, careful moves with their first encounter, this time was over far too fast, with only Nina's lingering, tempting smile to remind him what had just hit him.

He met her soft brown gaze and they both burst out laughing. With a shock, Jameson realized how little laughter had marked their life until then, despite the quiet joy that had built inside him day by day. When had he forgotten how to let go like this, how to relax with something as simple as laughter?

Too long ago. He'd let the excuse of sorrow and pain obliterate the giddiness from him. He'd needed to protect himself at Folsom, had had to guard every word, every careless emotion. But that was behind him now.

Jameson pressed a gentle kiss to her brow. "Be right back," he murmured before he went quickly into the bathroom to clean up. When he returned to the room, she held out her arms to him. He lay beside her again, her silky skin pressed against his, her head tucked under his chin.

They lay there together as the room darkened, the noise of the city filtering through the window. Jameson wanted badly to make love to her again, to feel himself inside her, her cries of passion in his ears. But magic seemed to hold them in its grasp, cushioning them with bliss, carving out a paradise for just the two of them. If he started touching her, kissing her, he was afraid that he would break the spell.

So he simply held her, listened to her breathing. Time passed, maybe an hour or more, but the enchantment made time unreal and unimportant. If he didn't move, he could stay here with her forever, never have to think beyond his next breath.

Finally, the most prosaic needs of his own body shattered the magic. His stomach rumbled with a hunger he'd tried to ignore and with a sigh, Nina said, "We should get up. Get something to eat."

No, not yet! his mind shouted, but the bewitchment had already slipped away. Nina moved from him, snapped on the light. For an instant, he was terrified that she'd vanish and take with her the bliss of the last few hours. But then she smiled down at him, her warm brown eyes meeting his. That much at least was real.

Nina ordered room service for them, both of them loath to leave the cozy sanctuary of their room. Feeling giggly and naughty, she hid naked in the bathroom while the bellboy delivered the food, then when Jameson gave her the all clear, insisted he take off his jeans again. They fell into bed for another breathless session of lovemaking, the food cooling on the table.

When they came up for air, they wolfed down the massive, nearly cold hamburgers and shared an outrageously expensive Caesar salad. They finished the sybaritic meal by feeding each other bites of dense, chocolate-mousse cake drizzled with pureed raspberries.

Too sated to move, Nina snuggled against Jameson in the bed, leaning against the headboard. He'd turned on the news, but although his gaze remained fixed on the screen, she doubted he was aware of the TV weatherman's storm warnings. She would have liked to think she was the distraction, but since they'd finished dinner, he'd begun to pull away from her, bit by bit. Not physically, but in a deeper, more elemental way.

She took his hand from his lap, sandwiching it between hers. "Did you want to spend the morning at the trade show tomorrow? Or should we pick up Nate and head back home?"

His gaze dropped to their linked hands and he gripped her more tightly. "Whatever you want."

She pressed her mouth to his shoulder. "We could stay here all morning. Checkout isn't until noon."

"If you want."

He wouldn't look at her, seemed even more distant than ever. Alarm panged in the pit of her stomach. "What do *you* want, Jameson?"

He slipped from the bed. "I need a shower."

A chill bit her more viciously than the cold San Francisco evening fog. She shivered as the bathroom door shut behind Jameson, then pulled the covers up to her chin.

The closeness had caught him off-guard, that was all. She'd had her own crisis earlier, the abandonment of the past haunting her, making her doubt her feelings. There was so much unsettled between her and Jameson, they both needed time to work out what to do next.

Her love for him still burned inside her, lit her way.

If she told him, wouldn't it make things easier? If he understood she was ready to commit herself to him, to their marriage? Surely it would make a difference.

She heard the shower shut off and threw aside the covers. Jittery, her nakedness no longer felt comfortable, and she dug in her travel bag for her nightgown. Pulling it on, she shut off the television and sat on the edge of the bed to wait for Jameson to emerge from the bathroom.

She rose as he strode into the room, a towel around his hips. "Jameson."

Strain tautened every line of his body. He reached for the remote and snapped the television on again. His broad back turned toward her, he faced the screen.

"Jameson," she called again.

"I'm tired." He stared at the TV. "Can it wait?"

His brusqueness shocked her. "I think we need to talk."

"About tomorrow?" He glanced at her sidelong. "I told you, whatever you want."

"About this afternoon. We should talk about that."

"We had sex." He pressed the off button on the remote. "Same as five years ago."

"There was more, Jameson. And that's what we need to talk about."

Now he turned toward her and his blue eyes seemed flat and dead. "Yeah, there was more. This time I was careful. This time there won't be any consequences."

He must have seen the agony in her face because color stained his cheeks. But he didn't say anything else, just tossed aside the remote and shut off his bedside light. Stripping the towel from his hips, he got into bed and lay facing the wall.

The cutting pain inside her wouldn't kill her, but her

heart felt shredded, her soul in tatters. The alien creature lying in that bed couldn't be Jameson. He'd been harsh, he'd been untouchable and even cold. But he'd never been as cruel as he'd been tonight.

Gasping in a breath, Nina grabbed her toiletries from her bag and headed for the bathroom. As she brushed her teeth and washed the tears from her face, she resolved to find a way past the stout walls Jameson had put up against her. Maybe not tonight or tomorrow, but surely someday love would batter them down.

Someday.

Chapter Thirteen

Jameson was studiously polite with her in the morning, carrying her bags down to the lobby, bringing the car up so she wouldn't have to walk down into the labyrinthine parking structure. Nina could see how his words from the night before were eating at him, she could see it in the desolate look in his eyes. Her forgiveness might soothe the guilt, ease the self-imposed load that weighted his shoulders. But it wasn't her forgiveness Jameson needed, it was his own.

She felt wounded as well and a childish part of her wanted to pout, to shut herself off from him. But that would wound her even more than simply putting aside the hurt of the night before. They would have to deal with it sooner or later if they had any hope of continuing on together. But she was willing to let it be later.

They stopped for breakfast at a coffee shop just outside the city, but Nina barely touched her pancakes and

Jameson picked at his omelette. Leaving the plates filled with food, they returned to his grandmother's house. The hour or so they visited after arriving at the palatial estate seemed endless, but Nina knew how key Lydia was to Jameson's past. If he and his grandmother could heal the rift between them, he could begin to heal himself. Then there might be a chance for a real marriage between him and Nina.

As they set out for home, thick black clouds gathered overhead, as if the skies sensed their turmoil. They'd barely reached Berkeley when the torrent began, angry, wind-whipped sheets of water dumping down. At times, the fall of rain was so heavy the windshield wipers couldn't keep up and Jameson had to slow to see through the thick streams of water.

What should have been a two-and-a-half hour trip stretched into a grueling four before they'd even reached Marbleville. Nate, not the best traveler on long trips, sat uncharacteristically quiet in the back seat, mustering up a wan smile when Nina turned to check on him. Jameson remained focused on his driving, sparing her only a quick glance when she brushed his shoulder to offer comfort.

They were finally past Marbleville and creeping up Interstate 80 for the final leg of the trip to Hart Valley when Nina's cell phone rang, the sound kicking her heart into high speed. Fumbling for the phone in her purse, she stabbed the answer button and gasped out a hello.

"Nina?" Her mother's voice faded into static. "…all okay?"

"You're breaking up, Mom." She waited for a response, heard none. "We're almost home."

"...home soon?" After another pause, her mother's voice came in more clearly. "Deer Creek is at flood stage. Mark and Beth Henley set up a sandbag brigade behind the inn."

"We'll be there in twenty minutes." She shut off the phone and relayed her mother's message to Jameson.

Nina's announcement set off a roiling in Jameson's stomach. He knew all too well the danger of small creeks flooding their banks. There'd been a brief scare five years ago when a storm cell had stubbornly stalled over Hart Valley. Deer Creek had risen dangerously high and they'd all been on alert throughout the night. Disaster had been averted when the storm finally moved on higher into the Sierras.

Squinting through the wash of water blurring the windshield, he spotted the Hart Valley exit up ahead. The storm seemed to intensify as they pulled off Interstate 80. "We'll have to drop Nate off at your folks."

"Of course. We'll go there first."

Jameson gave her a sidelong glance, trying to gauge her mood. He'd treated her monstrously last night, had been beyond cruel. He didn't even understand why, couldn't comprehend his own blind panic that had driven him to such ugly words. He'd been desperately afraid she'd tell him she'd had enough, that she and Nate were leaving him. The storm had provided the perfect diversion, although now that he knew about the flooding, he was ashamed of himself.

The thick fall of rain made the trip to Nina's parents' seem endless, although it was well within the twenty minutes she'd promised. Jameson popped the trunk so Nina could grab Nate's small bag, then he told his son to climb into the front seat. He gathered Nate up for the mad dash to the Russos' covered porch, Nina running along beside him. Once under cover, Mrs. Russo hugged Nina fiercely, then gave Jameson a peck on the cheek before taking her grandson from him.

"Beth says the inn is safe, but the water is nearly to the Gibbons' doorstep. Arlene is frantic."

With two sturdy rain ponchos provided by Mr. Russo, they hurried back to town. As he drove through the downpour, Jameson couldn't quite ignore the irony of the situation. Arlene Gibbons was the worst of the busybodies. She'd gone out of her way to tell him quite clearly he didn't belong—in Hart Valley or in Nina's and Nate's lives. Since that morning when she'd confronted him, she'd rarely turned up in the café when he was there, no doubt loath to spend any time in his company.

But none of that mattered. No matter how long Nina let him stay, he was part of her life now, which wove him firmly into the community of Hart Valley. He would help because that was what neighbors did. Whether it was the Gibbons or the Henleys or the Jarrets—he would lend a hand.

When Jameson parked on Main Street he saw that all the lights were off in the café. "Everyone must be on the brigade."

"We'd better get out there."

Despite the pressure of time, the need to join the others sandbagging the creek, Jameson stayed rooted to his seat. He and Nina had to talk, had to find a way through the tangle of hurt he'd built between them.

He met her gaze, put his hand to her cheek under the hood of the poncho. "Nina—"

"Later." She pulled his hand from her face and pressed a kiss to his palm. "We'd better go."

She turned away and opened the car door. He followed her lead, racing across the street. They found the others behind the public lot beside the Hart Valley Inn. Keith Delacroix, owner of the construction firm Jameson had worked for, had hauled in a load of sand and dumped it in the lot. Several men shoveled sand into bags held open by their wives or sisters, then a brigade ferried the filled sandbags to a growing barrier near the Gibbons house.

Tom Jarret handed Jameson a shovel, and Nina grabbed a gunnysack from a waiting pile. The rain pounded down while he methodically shoveled sand into bags, working beside the Jarrets, the Henleys and Mort and Arlene Gibbons. Caught up in the work at hand, Mort merely greeted him with a nod, while Arlene kept her gaze down on the sandbag in her hands. Once, when one of the several high school students dragged off his and the Gibbonses' bags at the same time, Arlene looked up at him. She opened her mouth as if to speak, then briskly turned away for another sack.

Nina worked tirelessly, dragging filled bags over to the brigade's start, taking a turn with the shovel when a breach in the sandbag barrier required Jameson to hurry over and help divert the water. When enough free hands were available to work, she darted across the street, bringing back the café's largest coffee urn and a supply of coffee. Once the coffee was brewing in the kitchen of the inn, she and Beth started up a brigade of their own making sandwiches from both the café and the inn's pantries and refrigerators.

At one point, it seemed all their efforts were for naught when the water lapped over the highest row of sandbags. The rain was pounding mercilessly, the black clouds seemed bent on squeezing every last drop of their moisture out. A filled sandbag under each arm, Jameson slogged through the rushing creek water, rocks and flotsam slamming into his ankles with each step. He and Tom Jarret got their bags in place just in time to prevent a worse breach, and moments later, the rain miraculously began to subside.

As he returned to the sand pile, Jameson caught Arlene looking his way. Her face was wet despite the hood of her rain jacket. Jameson realized it was tears rather than raindrops running down her furrowed cheeks.

He turned away, sure she wouldn't want him to know she was crying. But when he grabbed up his shovel, he felt someone thump on his back.

"Jameson O'Connell," Arlene said, her tone imperious but slightly frayed by tears.

Stabbing his shovel back in the sand, Jameson faced her. "Yes?"

Despite the obstinate set of her chin, he could see a thawing in her eyes. "Thank you." Turning on her heel, she strode back toward her house.

Hell had just been hit by an ice storm. He wouldn't be a bit surprised to see a porker flapping its wings through the now thinning rain. When he reached for his shovel again, he saw Nina coming toward him with a steaming paper cup, the smile on her face lifting him higher than that imaginary winged pig would have flown.

She handed over the coffee and he sipped it through the lid. It was hot and strong, warming his body even as Nina's quiet presence warmed his heart. He remembered the way he'd treated her last night and guilt cut through him, a reminder that a man with as many black sins on his soul didn't deserve a woman like Nina.

But she was his for now. He could drink in her smile, take as large a measure of her sweetness as he could before their time together ended. That dark blot on the horizon would just have to wait its turn.

She tipped her head toward Arlene, who now leaned against her husband out on their soggy front lawn. "I think you might have made a new friend."

"For now." Jameson emptied his cup and handed it back to her. "Tomorrow she'll remember what an SOB I am and she'll hate me again."

Nina's smile faded and despite the fading rain, it seemed an even thicker storm cloud had clotted overhead. "She's started to see who you really are—a good man. Why can't you see that?"

He grabbed a gunnysack and held it open while tossing in a shovelful of sand. "She's grateful we saved her house. That's pretty damned easy to see."

Nina stopped him from scooping up another shovelful. "I mean why can't you see what she sees? That you're a good man. Someone who's been through tough times and come out on the other side with his decency intact."

He couldn't bring himself to look at her. Pulling away, he muttered, "I have to fill another bag."

"It's not raining anymore, Jameson. The creek's gone

down." She gave him a shake. "You can stop pretending now."

Irritation lifted his gaze to hers. "Pretending what?"

"That you're still the bad boy."

She let go and marched away, head high. Jameson dropped his shovel, impulse pushing him to follow her. But he hadn't the slightest idea what he'd say in response to her preposterous statement.

In the glaring light of the public lot's flood lamps, he could see the borders of Deer Creek had retreated below the top of its banks. Shovels clattered as they were tossed back into pickup beds and someone had gathered up the remaining empty gunnysacks for the next crisis. Arlene and Mort held court on their front porch, shaking the hands of the last few stragglers before heading inside out of the chilly air.

Tom Jarret approached him across the parking lot. "I think that one's mine."

Jameson handed over the shovel and Tom checked the handle for the double J burned into the wood. "Thanks for the use of it."

"Thanks for your help," Tom said. "Arlene's a prickly old bird, but there's a kind heart buried under that crusty exterior."

Jameson laughed. "I'll take your word for it."

Tom lingered, idly twirling the shovel. "Looks like things are going well between you and Nina."

The plastic rain poncho suddenly felt too warm. Jameson unsnapped it and pulled it off. "Well enough, I suppose."

"Meaning what?" The rancher's blue eyes sharpened. "You'd better be here for the long haul, O'Connell."

Ire bubbled up inside Jameson, and he struggled against an old familiar urge take a poke at Tom. "That's none of your damn business."

"Nina and that little boy mean a lot to this town. To me in particular. That makes it my business."

He might have held back his fists, but Jameson realized there were more ways than physical violence to take a wrong step. "Look, I'm sorry. Nina and Nate…a man couldn't ask for better. But sometimes… Hell, it's so damn hard to do it right."

Now the rancher grinned. "That'll never change, O'Connell. Women are damned slippery. Kids…forget trying to figure them out. You just stick with them."

In that moment, there was nothing he wanted more. He just didn't know if it was in him to do it. "Thanks for the advice."

"Such as it is." Tom headed for his pickup where his wife, Andrea, waited. Halfway there, he turned back. "Your next day off, why don't you three come to dinner?"

"Sure. That would be great."

"I'll talk to Andy about it. She can give Nina a call." He continued on to his truck. After he threw the shovel into the bed, he gave his wife an enthusiastic kiss, then they climbed inside the truck.

After they'd pulled away, Jameson headed for the inn. As he pushed through the back door, J.C. Archer, owner of the town's bakery, passed him, raising a hand in greeting. "Good work, Jameson."

He didn't see Nina in the kitchen, so he continued on into the small dining room just beyond. He hadn't had much occasion to visit the Hart Valley Inn, other than the one or two times he'd come over to borrow supplies when the delivery trucks were delayed. The café would return the favor whenever the Henleys ran short, and the favors usually balanced out in the long run.

Nina and Beth Henley sat at the table where the inn-keeper served her guests breakfast, both with their feet up on a shared chair. Mark Henley stood leaning against a breakfront, a mug of coffee cradled in his hands. Beth glanced over at Jameson as he entered, then dropped her feet to the floor with a sigh.

"Mark, let's go to bed so these fine people can go home."

Mark took a last swig of his coffee. "Bed is right where I want you." He set the mug on the table.

Nina picked it up. "I'll rinse that on my way out."

As Mark nudged her toward the stairs, Beth looked back over her shoulder. "Lock the back door as you go out, please."

After they'd disappeared around the corner, Jameson heard Beth's giggle and Mark's answering growl. He caught a wistful look on Nina's face before she moved toward the kitchen.

He followed her, waiting until she'd emptied and rinsed the cup, then set it beside the dishwasher. After grabbing her poncho from a hook by the door, they locked the kitchen door behind them. Someone had cut the flood lamps and only the dim moonlight filtered through the remaining wisps of clouds to light their way back through the parking lot and across the street.

He threw her still wet poncho into the trunk with his, then opened her door, glad for the contact of her hand as he helped her inside. His exhaustion was bone deep, but if she'd asked him to leap from the car and run a marathon for her, he would have found the power to do it. He would have done that and more, just for one smile.

They drove the few miles to the house in silence. He knew he had to say something to her, had to find a way to heal the wounds he'd inflicted last night, but nothing that came to mind seemed at all sufficient. She deserved his best, more than his best, yet she so often got only the worst of him.

Finally he squeezed out the only three words he could think of to say. "Nina, I'm sorry."

She took a deep breath, let it out slowly. "Thank you."

As they pulled up their drive, he reached for her blindly. Fear spurted inside him that she would reject his touch, but she gathered up his hand, linked her fingers with his. An unfamiliar peace spread within him.

He stopped the car, taking back his hand long enough to shut off the engine. She reclaimed it, brought his fingers to her soft mouth and brushed a kiss against them. "They've begun to accept you, Jameson. You need to let them in."

Being a part of Hart Valley, when he'd always felt so outcast, would weave him even more inextricably into Nina's life. He knew he could not do one without the other. He knew as well that he wanted both—a shared life with Nina and to have this place be home for him at last.

Stopping long enough to get their bags, they went inside, lassitude weighting their steps. Without discussion, Nina walked alongside him to his room. They undressed, climbed into his bed, lay side by side with their arms around one another. His manhood was a brief intrusion, rising in response to her body pressed against his, but not even the temptation of Nina's sweetness could stir enough energy within him to follow through. He plummeted into sleep.

Nina awoke with a start the next morning, completely disoriented. A quick glance around reminded her that she'd slept in Jameson's room, in Jameson's arms. The rest of yesterday came back in blurred snatches of memory—the endless stormy drive back from the Bay Area, the flood, the desperate effort to save the Gibbons' house.

Jameson's side of the bed was empty, the sheets cold. That and the fragrance of coffee told her he'd been up long enough to brew a pot. But the house seemed still, so quiet she could hear the breeze sifting through the pines around the house. Maybe he'd gone outside to split wood for the fire. But she would have heard the blows of the ax, the creak of splitting wood.

A longing filled her—to spend their day off together, lingering over coffee and breakfast, sharing the contents of Monday's slim edition of the *Hart Valley Gazette*. She didn't know which Jameson she would face this morning—the generous, giving man she'd come to know in the past two months, or the cold, soulless one who had shown himself Saturday night. But if she just had time with him, she knew they could work through whatever darkness he still harbored inside himself.

She rose from the bed, every muscle screaming from yesterday's efforts. Jameson had retrieved her robe from her room and laid it across the foot of the bed, a sweet gesture. She wrapped it around her body, groaning as each ache manifested itself, then went in search of her clothes. She found her sweater and slacks readily enough, but her bra and panties were concealed by Jameson's T-shirt and her water-ruined socks and sneakers had somehow gotten shoved under the bed.

In her own room, she dressed quickly. As she crossed through the living room, she saw what she'd missed on her way to her bedroom—the Camry was missing from the drive. He'd left a brief, scribbled note on the kitchen island—*Gone to get Nate*—next to the coffeepot. Faintly disappointed that they wouldn't have the day alone, she sat at the island with a steaming cup of coffee to wait for him.

She'd barely skimmed the front page of the *Gazette* when she heard the crunch of tires on gravel. Nate dashed into the kitchen, red-cheeked from the cold, his dark hair windblown.

"Mommy, Mommy! Daddy took me to see the creek! He said there was a flood last night."

Jameson stood in the kitchen doorway, his face an enigma Nina couldn't decode. "Did Daddy tell you he helped to fight the flood?"

"No." Nate turned to his father, awestruck. "Did you, Daddy?"

Jameson handed Nate's small bag to his son. "Go on to your room and change."

Arms wrapped around his bag, Nate raced off. Jameson still hung back in the doorway. He'd pushed up the sleeves of his heather gray wool sweater, and the taut tendons in his hands revealed his tension.

Nina smiled, wishing he'd come to her, take her in his arms. "Thanks for bringing Nate home."

He crossed his arms over his chest, as if to put up a barrier against her. Frustration rose in Nina and she suppressed the urge to march over to him and give him a hard shake. "You went into town?"

Finally he pushed away from the doorway, but he gave her a wide berth as he headed for the coffeepot. "I thought I'd use today to catch up at the café." He poured himself a mug and took a swallow. "The compressor coils on the walk-in need cleaning, and I still need to add that shelf to the pantry."

"We'll go in with you—"

"No."

"But I've got some jobs I've been needing to get to. And Nate can help you in the pantry."

"The work will go quicker without Nate getting in the way."

"Maybe, but if we're together—"

"I can't have you with me."

Why not?

Jameson saw the question in her eyes. If she'd voiced it, he wasn't sure he would answer. How could he speak the words aloud—that he burned for her, that nothing more than a touch, the barest stroke of her fingers, would ignite the tinder of his passion. He couldn't go down that road again, not and keep his sanity intact. Because the time in her arms two days ago had wrapped her so tightly around his heart he thought he'd explode from the unfamiliar emotion bursting inside him.

He wanted her so keenly—as his wife, as the mother of his son, as a lover in his bed—that he could not bear to think of the two-year limit they'd placed on their time together. Even if they hadn't set that limit, he'd come to the realization he would likely find a way to destroy their marriage anyway. If not by committing the same sins his father had, he would certainly fail her through some other weakness.

So he had to keep his distance from her. Only that would keep the darkness from swallowing him up when she left him…as she inevitably would.

She slid from her stool, starting toward him. He shook his head and her name came out roughly. "Nina—"

"Talk to me, Jameson."

"There's nothing to talk about." He lied. There was so much inside, he was terrified there would be nothing left of him if he expressed it.

"Why did you shut yourself down Saturday night? Why were you so cruel?"

A fist of guilt punched his gut. "I can't do this, Nina."

She laid her hands on his shoulders, rubbed soothingly. "Let me in. Please."

He couldn't. If he did, he'd be lost, so tied to her he'd be destroyed when she left. He had to find a way to put the barriers up between them again, to sever the connections that persisted in joining each time she touched him.

Pulling away, he slammed his mug to the counter, the scald of coffee on his hand a welcome distraction. "I might not be back for dinner." He strode away from her and out of the kitchen.

He felt sick as he drove back into town, the black coffee sitting badly in his empty stomach. He'd have to grab something to eat at the café, although the thought of food nauseated him even more.

His body throbbed, clamoring for Nina, an ache that encompassed his entire self. He could be in her arms at that moment, could draw her sweetness in close to him, let it heal even the most clandestine wounds. He could allow himself those few moments of the paradise that was Nina.

But that happiness would only make the torture of eventually losing her that much more agonizing. Wasn't it better to deny himself now to ease that pain later?

He parked back behind the café and let himself in the back door. Exhaustion lay heavily on his shoulders, weighted his footsteps. He didn't know how he'd get the energy to complete even the simple tasks he'd set for himself.

The jingle of the front door brought him out of the kitchen, ready to tell whoever had entered that the café was closed. A moment before he saw Nina, he remembered the front door was locked and only she could have let herself in. He saw her little used sedan parked out front, saw Nate running past her, his little arms outstretched for a hug.

"We came to help, Daddy!"

As he grabbed up Nate, Jameson's heart squeezed tight, then seemed to expand to fill his chest. "That's great. I'm glad you're here."

He set his son down, then met Nina's soft brown gaze. Her smile filled up the last few empty places inside him. When she moved toward him, he welcomed her in his embrace.

For now, he chose paradise.

Chapter Fourteen

The Saturday morning breakfast rush was still in full swing when Jameson had his third meltdown of the day. Nina had brought another thirty-six-count flat of eggs from the walk-in and slid it onto the prep counter just as Jameson turned to set down a skillet full of ham scramble. She tried to rescue the three-dozen eggs, but couldn't scoot them clear before the hot skillet crushed half the flat. Jameson's shouted expletive as he snatched the skillet back nearly brought the rafters down.

Nate, squirreled away in his cubby with a video, came running to see what was up and nearly collided with the hot pan. When Jameson put out a hand to protect his son, he scorched his arm on the skillet, generating another string of curses.

"Nate!" he roared as he slammed the pan onto a clear spot on the counter. "Get your butt back in your cubby!"

Nate looked close to tears as he skittered back and

ran off. Nina suppressed a compulsion to toss the ham scramble at Jameson, burned arm or no burned arm. But before she could have a few choice words with her husband, he stomped off into the back and out the rear door.

Reining in her temper, Nina quickly scooped the scramble onto the plate waiting for them, rescued the hash browns from the griddle and served up the order with an orange slice garnish. Lacey, who'd been standing on the other side of the pass-through waiting for the last plate, gave Nina an encouraging smile before she headed out to deliver the food.

With the wild storm of a week ago, ski season was in full swing. Nina's Café had gained a reputation in recent years as the place to stop on the way to Lake Tahoe's North Shore ski resorts. With the ski crowd competing with the usual locals coming in for Saturday morning breakfast, the café was bursting at the seams.

Nina had thought she and Jameson had reached a turning point last Monday. They'd felt like a real family as they worked together in the quiet café, Nate handing Jameson tools as he caught up on various fix-it tasks, Nina repainting the dry-stores area her son and husband had helped her empty. They'd taken a break while the paint dried, indulging in elaborate custom sandwiches like turkey, cream cheese and cranberries on whole wheat and Nate's stomach-churning combo of hamburger and peanut butter.

After an afternoon spent restocking the dry-store shelves and giving the walk-in a thorough cleaning, they drove down to Marbleville for a movie and a light dinner. When they returned home and put a zonked out Nate to bed, Jameson kissed her passionately in the kitchen, a prelude, Nina thought, to lovemaking. But he walked her to her own bedroom, kissed her and said good-night, leaving her aching for his touch and completely confused.

As the week wore on, Jameson grew ever more distant and increasingly irritable. He seemed intent on pushing her farther and farther away, as if to reestablish the boundaries and secret walls he'd maintained when he'd first reappeared in Hart Valley. It was as if he was doing his best to alienate himself from her and Nate, to pull away from them.

Why? She'd asked herself that question more than once. Although their promised two years were nowhere near completion, maybe he'd had enough. Maybe he preferred keeping his walls around him.

Maybe he intended to leave.

This morning, he'd already snapped at Lacey when she'd returned with scrambled eggs that should have been sunny-side up and a side of bacon that should have been sausage. Then when Nate couldn't decide between pancakes and French toast, Jameson had slapped a box of cold cereal in Nate's hands, leaving Nina to deal with their tearful son. After that, the café crowd reached crisis level and it was all she and Jameson could do to get the food cooked and served.

Nina had just finished up Jameson's order when he returned to the kitchen looking no less stormy than when he left it. Without a word he transferred the unbroken eggs from the half-ruined flat to the bowl kept by the stove and dumped the soggy cardboard in the trash. Then he grabbed the now-cooled skillet to clean the mess of congealed egg from its bottom.

As he returned from the back with the washed pan, he wouldn't meet her gaze. She planted herself in his path, but he dodged her, heading toward the electric slicer where a hunk of ham waited to be cut into steaks. He flipped on the slicer and fed the ham across the razor-sharp blade, moving the thick ovals to a waiting stainless-steel square.

"Order up," Lacey called from the other side of the window.

Nina reached for the order slip. "I'll get it."

Jameson didn't so much as acknowledge her offer. His jaw muscle flexed, as if he barely contained something inside him. Nina thought she would scream with not knowing what he was thinking, what he was feeling. She was going to have to have things out with him, even if he truly did intend to leave her and Nate.

She cooked up Lacey's large order by rote, so habituated to the café's unchanging menu she barely had to think. A plate of scrambled eggs, another with over easy. Denver omelette stuffed with ham, peppers and cheese, Hangtown fry dotted with bacon and oysters. When she took the last slice of orange from its plastic storage container, Jameson had another filled container ready for her. He took great care not to touch her as he handed the oranges over.

As she put up the last plate, customers were backed up at the register, waiting to pay. She went out front to ring them up, refilled four coffees at the counter, then leaned back against the pass-through when she saw the dining room had nearly emptied. Other than the large table Lacey was just finishing up and the few locals at the counter, they had some breathing space.

But she'd scarcely had a chance to take a breath before potential trouble jangled its way inside the café. Arlene Gibbons, her fellow three busybodies in tow, marched toward Nina, head held high.

As imperious as a queen, Arlene issued her command. "I'd like to see your husband, please, Nina."

Nina glanced back at Jameson through the pass-through and unease roiled inside her. As testy as he'd been this morning, all he needed was Arlene's snappish disapproval to set off another explosion. Nina studied Jameson's face, his hooded blue gaze, and tried to unravel what might be going on inside of him. But she couldn't read him.

He tugged off his apron, which seemed to Nina the equivalent of rolling up his sleeves in preparation for a fight. Arlene was giving nothing away, either, the lines of her seventy-year-old face as formidable as Jameson's more youthful one.

Behind Arlene, Frida Wilkins, Harriet Mason and Georgia Haynes stood shoulder to shoulder. If she hadn't been so on edge from Jameson's moody, erratic behavior this week, Nina would have laughed at the strange twist on *High Noon* that was unfolding before her.

Jameson planted his hands on the counter opposite Arlene, leaning forward a bit in challenge. "You wanted to see me?"

Arlene's nose tipped even higher in the air. "I'm here to apologize."

Jameson had expected another diatribe from Arlene Gibbons and had ready any number of pithy responses. Damned if he'd let that skinny little old lady tell him where he belonged, never mind that he'd begun to believe her nasty words.

When she instead delivered an apology, he was struck dumb. As his brain scrambled to regroup, he became aware of Nina's hand on his arm and he sensed her stalwart support for him. Not that he deserved it, considering how he'd been treating her this week.

But he didn't understand the emotions that had been churning in him the past several days any more than he comprehended Arlene's unexpected mea culpa. He decided to keep his mouth shut and see what else the old busybody had to say. No point in making anything easier for her.

"You were a crazy wild boy, always into trouble. Your father had a little bit to do with that, but you can't put it all on your daddy, no matter what kind of snake he was."

They were back to the old Arlene. Jameson took an impatient step back. "I have work to do."

"Hold on!" When he continued on toward the kitchen, Arlene followed her haughty edict with a hasty "Please."

He wasn't the least bit inclined to let the old girl order him around. But when Nina tugged his arm and with only a look asked him to stay and listen, he couldn't possibly refuse. "Go on."

"You've turned your life around, I can see that," Arlene said, a trace more kindness in her tone. "You've made a decent husband for Nina, you're good with your son. That's your mother's influence."

He had to tamp down a spurt of anger. "What do you know about my mother?"

"More than you'd think, Jameson O'Connell." She

tossed her head. "I'm acquainted with your grandmother, did you know that? We attended Mission High School together."

Unease tickled inside him and on its heels came the sudden urge to derail whatever Arlene had in mind to say next. "Apology accepted, Mrs. Gibbons. I have to get back—" Nina's hand tightened on his arm and he froze.

Like a freight train, revelation thundered toward him in the shape of a seventy-year-old lady. "I called Lydia after you showed up in town, to warn her you were out of prison. She certainly gave me an earful."

He sensed rather than heard Nina's sudden intake of breath. Expectation sang along his veins, tingling where her hand lay against his arm.

Oblivious, Arlene roared on. "I know what happened that night. How you tried to save your brother—darn fool stupid, if you ask me." Now she turned to Nina. "He's a good man, but even the best put so much stock into being noble, they forget who they leave behind. Don't you let him."

He felt each finger of Nina's hand, distinct, as she tightened her grip. "I won't."

Now the old busybody turned to her entourage. "This boy is part of our community. No one is to treat him any different."

With nods and affirmations, the small group turned away and headed for their usual table by the front window. Jameson stood there in the aftermath, Nina beside him with questions brewing, ready to pop out like quills off a porcupine.

She let go of his arm, arranged her hands carefully at her sides. "Come in the back with me."

He couldn't imagine refusing. All the reasons he'd kept to himself the details of that night with Sean seemed trivial and self-serving. What had been so clear just a few minutes ago now seemed muddied with self-indulgent pride.

They went back to Nate's cubby where their son had been quietly coloring as he watched a video. When Nina switched off the television and stopped the DVD, Nate looked up from his crayons.

Nina urged the boy from his chair. "Go out front, sweetie. Ask Lacey for a glass of milk and some of that apple pie."

Nate glanced up at him and for an instant Jameson felt a certain male kinship with his son. Even Nate knew his daddy was in trouble with his mommy.

Nina waited until he'd gone, then took a breath. "Tell me."

His throat went dry and he could barely get the words out. "I wasn't driving."

She stared at him a moment before understanding kicked in. "The night that woman was killed…you weren't driving the car?" He nodded. "Sean was?"

The truth was supposed to make you free, but his admission lay like a stone in his belly. "Sean was behind the wheel, but I'm just as guilty."

Nina shook her head. "I don't understand how."

The small space of Nate's cubby seemed impossibly confining. "I should have found a way to keep him from driving. I took his keys when we were in the bar. I didn't know he had a spare in his wallet."

The memories rushed back—Sean disappearing into the bathroom, gone for far too long. The roar of Sean's souped-up Camaro as he gunned the engine. The way the distance between him and the hot-red car seemed endless.

Nina waited, expectant. "Tell me," she said again.

Swiping his hand over his face, Jameson struggled with the words. "No way to stop him. Barely made it inside as it was. My ankle…think I sprained it jumping in the car as he drove off."

It all spilled out then—how his brother blocked his every effort to switch off the engine before they left the parking lot. The way he grabbed the wheel again and again to keep Sean in his lane as he sped down the road. His brother's wild sucker punch that knocked him for a loop, giving Sean enough time to drift into oncoming traffic.

That one image—of the mother's face as the Camaro hurtled toward them—had etched itself so deeply into his brain he could never shake it loose. A doctor had told him later the glare of headlights would have made it impossible to see through the windshield of the other car, but somehow that ghost memory persisted.

Still caught up in the old nightmare, he wasn't aware at first of Nina's hands on his face, her sweet voice speaking soothingly. "It wasn't your fault. You did everything you could."

He shook his head in denial. "I should have stopped him. That was why…it was easy to take the blame. Because I should have taken care of Sean, kept him out of trouble. That mother and her child died because I couldn't."

Nina bent his head down, her brown eyes severe. "She died because your brother drove drunk. You did everything you could to stop him." Her hands moving to his shoulders, she gave him a shake, harder than he would have expected from a woman as small as her. "You did everything you could!"

Her conviction lapped at him, like small waves kissing a protected cove. "I tried to save him," he said roughly.

"Yes." Her soft voice was a balm.

"I think…he didn't want to be saved." That insight sent grief coursing through him.

Gathering up his hands, she pressed them to her mouth. "How did you get out of prison?"

"My brother…" His throat felt tight with tears, and he hadn't cried since his mother died. "He had AIDS. He contracted it from a dirty needle shooting up. He hadn't told anyone, wouldn't take care of himself. When he caught pneumonia, my grandmother put him in the hospital, too damn late. Near the end, he told her."

"So she got you released."

With a shock, he realized his resentment at his grandmother's intervention had vanished. "She hired an attorney, had my brother deposed at the hospital. The judge was a friend of my grandfather's, but it was straight up. Within a month I was out."

"She loves you, Jameson. You have to see that."

Deep inside him, a part of his soul wanted to deny it. But wasn't it time he let go of that?

As release washed through him, quiet joy filling his heart, he put his arms around his wife. This was all that mattered—Nina, the woman he'd made a child with, the woman he'd built his life around.

"Jameson?" Her breath whispered in his ear. She

pushed back from him, gazed up at him with a solemn expression. "I need you to know…"

Panic exploded inside him—she couldn't stay with him any longer, she wanted him out of her life and Nate's. He wanted to cover her mouth with his hand, stop her words. But she spoke before he could so much as move.

"I love you, Jameson."

The words punched the air from his lungs and his brain came to a dead stop. An inexplicable fear slammed into him, pushing him away from Nina. In terror's grip, he stumbled out of Nate's cubby and blindly toward the café's rear door.

She called his name as he headed for the car, but he focused instead on his footsteps scraping on gravel, on the damp December air soaking through his T-shirt. Inside the Camry, he pushed the key in the ignition with shaking hands. A voice inside him, untouched by the irrational fear, told him to stop being an idiot, to go back to his wife. Gunning the engine, he blocked logic from his mind and drove away.

He got as far as the end of Main Street when he realized with a shock he was headed toward home. In all the years he'd run away to escape his father's fists, he'd always sought out a number of hiding places he'd found, sanctuary against his father's wrath. But the crazy fear that Nina's words had started up in him had driven him instead to the place they'd built together. A place they'd begun to fill with love.

There was no other sanctuary. Every other escape route led to loneliness and isolation and anguish. He'd been able to bear it as a boy because he didn't know anything better. What excuse did he have now for choosing darkness?

Pulling the Camry over into the empty lot next to Archer's Bakery, Jameson fished in the glove compartment for his cell phone. Dialing the café, he figured he could do at least one thing right.

Nina answered, breathless, without the usual café greeting. "Jameson?"

His heart soared at the sound of her voice, but the grip of uncertainty pulled it back down. "I need a little time."

She hesitated and the silence dug inside him. He heard the careful neutrality in her tone. "There's probably an hour before the lunch rush starts."

"I'll be back before then."

He hung up the phone and tossed it back in the glove compartment, then hunched down in his seat. Two paths lay before him. He could battle his fears and find a way to accept Nina's love, even if he couldn't return it. Or he could save them all the anguish of the battle by walking away.

The first path seemed unreachable, the second impossible to even consider. But as a picture of Nate's face swam into his consciousness, the hurt in his innocent brown eyes when Jameson had shouted at him, guilt burrowed deep. Maybe it would be better if he stepped out of their lives. What kind of father was he anyway to be as cruel to his son as he had been? And what if the harsh words became physical blows? He felt sick at the prospect.

He pulled the car back onto Main Street and continued toward home. He probably wouldn't be able to reach the attorney on a Saturday, but he could at least call and leave a message on his voice mail. He'd wanted to transfer his grandmother's trust to Nate anyway; if he put things in motion now, he could be ready when he made his choice, whichever direction he went.

Desolate, he headed for home.

At a quarter past eleven, Nina sat with Nate at the front booth, trying to focus on a dairy invoice as her son read a simple picture book. Lacey sat at the front counter with her feet up on the next chair over, flipping through a women's magazine. The café was momentarily empty of customers.

Arlene and her cronies had finally cleared out ten minutes ago. They'd lingered so long at their table, Nina had to squelch the urge several times to demand they leave. Arlene might have had no way of knowing Jameson had gone—let alone what had driven him away—but every time Nina looked her way, she saw speculation in the shrewd old woman's gaze. She could just imagine what Arlene was thinking.

The anger Nina had felt when Jameson walked away from her bubbled up again and the edges of the dairy invoice crumpled in her hands. She set the papers down and took a breath. He'd called her this time, almost immediately after he left. Despite the intense emotions set off when she'd told him she loved him, he'd brought himself to pick up the phone and talk to her. He'd assured her he'd be back. He hadn't left her hanging this time.

Leaning back in the booth, she stretched her tired muscles, slipping off her flats to wriggle her toes. She'd have to get up soon and finish the prep for lunch. Before she sat down, she'd returned the eggs, bacon and sausage to the walk-in and brought out the sliced turkey, ham and roast beef. The quiche for the lunch special still needed to be sliced and she ought to open another can of cranberries for the hot turkey sandwich plate. But she wanted to wait just a few more minutes, until Jameson returned. She'd rather get the air cleared before resuming work.

She heard the rear door bang shut and within her relief warred with irritation. Putting her hand over Nate's, she waited until he looked up at her. "You can stay out here until Lacey needs the table."

Nate's gaze strayed from hers. A glance over her shoulder told her Jameson stood in the kitchen doorway. Nate's brow furrowed. "Is Daddy still mad?"

Anger returned. Bad enough Jameson walked away, but when his behavior added to Nate's anguish, Nina had to draw the line. She could give her husband space to work out issues troubling him, but when it came to their son, he'd darn well better act like an adult.

"If Daddy's mad, it is absolutely not your fault. He just has a few problems to solve." She shot another quick look over her shoulder. "Mommy's going to help him."

She rose and marched over to Jameson. A hand planted on his chest, she backed him into the kitchen, then turned him around and escorted him to the rear door. Snagging their jackets, she pushed him outside, then shut the door behind them.

She tossed him his jacket, then pulled on her own. "Let's take a walk," she said, gesturing down the gravel drive that ran behind the businesses along the south side of Main Street. He fell in beside her.

She wanted to get the worst of it out of the way, but

her heart thundered and her throat closed as she tried to frame the question. It came out barely louder than a whisper. "Jameson...do you want to leave?"

She glanced over at him and something flickered in his face that alarmed her. He turned away, the emotion hidden again. "No."

She ought to press the issue, ferret out what lay behind his perfunctory response. But she feared what she might find out.

Instead, she redirected her focus on their son. "You can't treat Nate the way you did today. Vent your anger on me, not him."

"You don't deserve it either, Nina."

"I don't. But it cuts Nate much deeper than it does me. You have to apologize."

His face set, he nodded. "I will."

He fell silent. There was more to be said, but she wanted him to say it without her prodding. So she waited, listening to the crunch of gravel under their feet, the wind rocking the branches of the pines. The breeze carried the yeasty fragrance of fresh bread from Archer's bakery another block down. Maybe they could stop in and buy a still-warm loaf. She and Jameson could sit down with it, share it as they worked through the stumbling blocks that seemed to litter their way together.

Why couldn't it be that simple?

"Nina..." His foot struck a rock, sent it tumbling along the drive. "What you said..."

"I won't take it back, Jameson." She said the words lightly, but her stomach clenched.

"I should be able to say it, too, I should be able to—"

"No shoulds, Jameson." She took his hand, bringing him to a stop as she turned him toward her. "I said it because I had to. Because the words wouldn't stay inside any longer."

He enfolded her hand in his and she saw a desperation in his gaze. "You and Nate…you're my world. But sometimes I don't know how to feel."

He looked up at the pale blue sky, tension in his jaw. "My father…when the world didn't go his way, when he was angry or hurting or sad…"

She raised her free hand to his cheek, his beard-roughened skin warm against her palm. "He used his fists."

He traced the path of a hawk with his turbulent blue gaze. "On my mother, then on me. You know what the shrinks say about the sons of abusers."

"Jameson." She waited until he lowered his gaze to her. "You would never hit Nate or me. I know that."

"There have been times, times when I felt so close to…" He shut his eyes as if to reject the ugly possibility. "It's better if I leave."

Better if I leave.

Unease rippled inside her. "You mean walk away for a while. Get some breathing room."

He opened his eyes again. "Yes. That's what I mean."

She gave his hand a squeeze. "As long as you always come back."

He studied her face, as if committing it to memory. Then he drew her in his arms, holding her tightly, the heat from his body warming her clear to her toes. He covered her mouth with his, and his hot kiss promised an even hotter passion.

His mouth close to her ear, his whispered words chased the last of the December chill. "Let's close early tonight."

Even as she murmured a fervent, "Yes," she couldn't shake the sense that something was terribly wrong.

Chapter Fifteen

The afternoon seemed endless. Where before Jameson had seemed intent on avoiding contact with her, now he found excuses to brush against her. Fingertips across the back of her hand as he took a plate from her, his shoulder grazing her breast when he reached past her for a baked potato. Desire coiled inside her, like smoke from a burning ember, hot and heady.

There was an edge to his touch that worried her, an urgency that went beyond simple passion. As the dinner rush ground on toward the promised early closing time, Nina caught him staring at her, the intensity in his blue eyes sending a message she couldn't decipher. Even as she looked forward eagerly to time alone with him, she longed to discover what he held so tightly inside himself.

He'd settled things with Nate first thing, taking him back in the cubby to apologize the moment they returned to the café. Not wanting to eavesdrop, Nina only heard the rumble of Jameson's words, then their son's high childish voice. She couldn't resist a peek inside the cubby and saw Jameson pick up Nate and hold him close.

Patting his father's cheek, Nate smiled sweetly. "I love you, Daddy."

Nina went still as she waited for Jameson's response. Surely he wouldn't walk away as he'd done to her.

There was no hesitation in his reply. "I love you, too, Nate."

He swung Nate down to the floor again and caught sight of her standing outside the cubby. Whatever emotions might be tumbling inside of him he concealed with the heat of his gaze. He closed the distance between them and kissed her so briefly, she thought she'd die without another touch. When he'd tossed her a smile over his shoulder as he'd returned to the kitchen she wanted to punch him—then wrestle him into bed.

But as the evening wore on, the fleeting playfulness of that moment vanished. Although the heat remained, ratcheting up as the time crawled on to eight o'clock, she felt the barriers again. She would have his body again tonight, but would he give her more than that?

Jameson nearly chased the last customers from the café, bringing the check with the last of their food, clearing the table when they'd barely finished. He locked the door after them, then they cleaned up and rang out in record time. Nate was giddy with excitement that they were heading home early and he extracted a promise from his father of two bedtime stories.

Jameson took his time with the stories, snuggling with Nate after Nina had given him his bath, acting out all the parts. Nina sat in Nate's red vinyl beanbag chair, enjoying the sound of Jameson's voice, relishing the anticipation of being in his arms.

While Jameson tucked Nate in, Nina fetched a glass of water and set it on the nightstand. As Jameson waited in the doorway, she knelt by Nate's bed.

"Sweetie…" She swept Nate's hair back from his brow. "If you wake up during the night, I'll be in Daddy's room."

"Okay." He turned over and burrowed under his covers. "G'night."

Nina switched off the bedside light, leaving only the night-light glowing. Jameson put his hand out to her and she rose, crossing the room to him. Linked only by their hands, they headed down the hall to his room, turning off lights as they went.

He drew her into his room, then into his arms, a dimmed lamp in the corner illuminating the lines of his face. Heated by the afternoon and evening's teasing, she'd expected a frantic first coupling. But for long moments he just gazed down at her. Sadness flickered in his eyes, then was gone again, making her doubt what she'd seen.

"Jameson," she whispered, "What—"

He lowered his head to hers, cutting off her query with a kiss. One hand tangled in her hair, the other at her waist, he sipped at her mouth, tasted her with gentle forays of his tongue. His hold on her was almost tentative, as if she were delicate crystal, liable to break. This was different from San Francisco, when their slow union increased their passion. Now it seemed Jameson feared she would evaporate if he wasn't careful.

She pulled back, cupped his face with her hands. "Jameson," she murmured, "I'm not going anywhere."

She saw the sadness again, just a trace of it before he pressed his lips against hers again. Angling her toward the bed, he sat at the foot and tugged her between his knees. His fingers worked under the hem of her sweater, dragging it up her rib cage. Thumbs grazing her breasts as he pulled the sweater off, he tossed it aside before burying his face in her soft cleavage. His tongue dove into the warm valley, and the wet heat stole her breath.

He unbuttoned her slacks, lowered the zipper, then skimmed them off her. Scooting back, he urged her onto his lap and she straddled him. His jeans were rough on the insides of her thighs, his manhood a hard ridge pressing against her. She tipped her hips toward him and his soft groan skittered up her spine.

He slipped her bra straps from her shoulders, then reached back to unhook the clasp. Her breasts felt heavy and swollen, achingly sensitive. When his palms brushed against her nipples, the sensation dove straight through her body, escalating at the vee of her legs. She squirmed against him, too restless to be still. She felt on the edge of climax with just the touch of his hands on her breasts.

Wanting to feel more of him, she freed his T-shirt from his jeans and pulled it over his head. The contact of her breasts against his bare chest was indescribable, moving her even closer to bliss. The muscles of his back rippled under her hands as his arms wrapped around her, his mouth on hers again. His tongue thrust inside her mouth in a familiar rhythm, and unbearable heat ignited within her.

He turned, stretching out on the bed and bringing her with him. He shoved off jeans and shorts, then slid her panties from her hips. As he reached for a condom in the nightstand drawer, Nina wanted to stop him. She'd never thought of another child, felt complete with just Nate, but in that moment another baby, one whose life she could share with Jameson, seemed so right.

But it was a decision they would both have to make, one they would have plenty of time to discuss. So she waited while he sheathed himself, then pulled her close. His hands on her, touching her everywhere, her breasts, her hips, the moist folds between her legs, urged her nearer and nearer the precipice. A finger deep inside her, he drove her to climax, her body bursting into a million sparks, tumbling into space.

She still throbbed with sensation when he pressed her back and nudged between her legs. He entered her with a deep thrust, his body taut. Her hands on his hips, she urged him to move, gratified when he rocked against her. She peaked again, the orgasm centered deep in her body, a lingering ecstasy that startled her into a soft scream. He reached his peak soon after, his power spilling into her, filling her with joy.

When they'd both returned to reality, he shifted, taking his weight off her. He lay with his face nuzzling her neck, his hand on her breast, idly stroking. Then with a sigh and a kiss, he rose and headed for the adjoining bathroom. By the time he'd cleaned up and returned, Nina had crawled under the covers. Drawing back the blankets, she invited him to lie beside her again. He switched off the corner light, then headed for the bed.

The furnace cycled on as he settled beside her, but she only needed Jameson's heat to keep her warm. In the darkness, she couldn't see his face, could only sense his mood from the feel of his body. The lassitude from their lovemaking had disappeared so quickly, it was clear he was still troubled.

"Jameson," she whispered into the darkness. "What's the matter?"

Silence beat out a pattern in her ears in cadence with her heartbeat. She thought he wouldn't answer and had taken a breath to ask again when he finally spoke. "I don't want to lose you."

"You won't, Jameson. I won't leave you."

"I promised you two years."

"Then I absolve you of the promise."

She thought that would relieve his tension, instead he stiffened in her arms. "I would never leave him behind, Nina. I couldn't."

His fervency set off a faint claxon inside her. "Of course not. I would never expect you to."

"I have to be a different man than my father." His voice seemed constricted. "Leaving Nate behind will never be part of that."

His cryptic words confused her, increased her sense of alarm. "There are no limits to our marriage, Jameson. No need for you to ever leave."

Another long pause, then he pressed a kiss to the top of her head. "No limits."

Then his hands moved again, all along her body, goading her into passion again. The unanswered questions dispersed, dissolved by heat and the brightness of desire.

* * *

Nina sleepwalked through most of Sunday, feeling bleary-eyed, but delightfully debauched and disheveled. When the alarm had gone off far too early, Jameson had shut it off and told her to stay put, that he'd open up. She'd reset the alarm and nestled back under the covers, a sense of well-being suffusing her.

She'd arrived at the café mid-morning after taking Nate over to her parents' house. Her mother planned to take her grandson down to Marbleville so she could help him with his Christmas shopping. No doubt Nate would return with one or two early Christmas toys himself since his generous grandma couldn't resist indulging him.

By late afternoon, Nina was desperate for a nap, preferably with Jameson at her side. She sat sideways in the front booth, feet up, with last month's ring-outs spread on the table. She liked to compare the previous year with the current one, to keep track of sales from year to year. But her mind kept wandering to the man working in the kitchen and the numbers on the sheets swam into incomprehensible squiggles.

She yawned, her gaze straying to the clock. Although the café was empty, the dinner hour was quickly approaching. She wanted nothing more than to close up and go home to enjoy a quiet dinner with her husband and son before tumbling into bed again.

She caught Jameson staring at her through the order window and she smiled, hoping to lure him out of the kitchen. He'd been oddly distant all day, not avoiding her so much as preoccupied. Although yesterday's tension had eased, he seemed to be wrestling with something, working something out in his mind.

She crooked a finger at him and when he headed for her, she slid her feet from the booth seat. She pulled him in beside her and had time for one brief kiss before the front door jingled. Nate thundered in, a plastic carrying case in one hand, a large pad of art paper in the other. His grandma entered at a more sedate pace, smiling at her grandson's antics.

"Mommy, look what Grandma got me!" He slammed the big pad on top of her sales reports and a few fluttered to the floor.

Jameson put out a hand to slow down his son. "Nate, careful. Pick up Mommy's papers."

"Sorry, Mommy." He quickly scrambled on the floor as Jameson relocated the art pad to another table. Once Nate had replaced the rumpled reports, he opened up the art pad, then the large plastic box of pencils and charcoals. Perched on his knees on a chair, he started to draw.

"If you'll excuse me," Nina's mother said, "this boy has me worn to a nubbin." Once she'd gone, Jameson sat back down with Nina, fingers linked with hers.

As he gazed over at his son, he brought her hand up to his lips and held it there. He spoke so softly, she could barely hear the words. "You're everything to me."

That should have comforted her, eased her. But he wouldn't look at her and she felt the edginess in him again.

Pulling her hand free, she raised it to his face, turning him toward her. She waited until his eyes met hers, put every ounce of conviction she could in her voice. "I love you, Jameson."

When he tried to look away, she wouldn't let him, keeping her hand against his cheek. "Whatever you feel, it's enough. I know that. You don't have to call it love, because it will bond us all the same."

His lips curved in a faint smile. "I wish I could be as sure as you."

Jameson took Nina's hand, brought it to his lips. As he pressed a kiss into her palm, he relished her warmth, her sweetness. Last night had been both rapturous and agonizing, reminding him again of what he would leave behind if he walked away. Not just the mind-blowing passion, but Nina's complete devotion.

If only he could possess her conviction that what he felt for her was enough. If only his conscience wasn't screaming at him that she deserved something more—a man who loved her, who could be depended on to keep her safe, both from the world's evils and from his own weaknesses.

Giving her hand another kiss, he pulled away. "It's nearly five. I should get back to the kitchen."

When he rose, she slid from the booth as well. "I'll come back with you."

Nate's growl stopped them both. His face set with determination, their son was crisscrossing the picture he'd drawn with the obliterating strokes of a black charcoal. Then he ripped the page from the pad and tossed it aside. The sheet fluttered to the floor.

Nina bent to see the now-ruined drawing. "Sweetheart, what was wrong with the picture?"

Nate was already busy with another artwork. "Didn't like it."

To Jameson's eye, the rejected drawing didn't look much different than some of Nate's other masterpieces. "Maybe you could have fixed it."

"Nope." Nate scrawled long jagged lines with a red pencil. "Wanted to start over."

Start over. The words resonated inside Jameson. If only there was a way to start himself over, reset his life, wipe away the ugliness the same way Nate had blotted his picture out with the charcoal.

An image erupted in his mind of the stark, bleak cabin he'd grown up in, the dark symbol of a childhood of aching loneliness. So many tears were wept in that dismal place; so much sorrow haunted its rooms. In some ways those time-strafed walls had been more a prison than Folsom.

Start over. Hadn't Nina given him exactly that chance with her love, with the home she shared with him? And Nate—what better way to be reborn than through a child? He'd missed so many years of his son's life, but he had the chance to experience every moment of Nate's future.

With the brilliance of a supernova, the idea came to him. A way to put away the past, to liberate his soul. A way to discover if inside him he had an answer to Nina's declaration of love.

He imagined walls shattering, coming down, all the old ugliness cleaned away. The fist of fear he'd harbored inside of himself since he'd decided to leave now loosened, eased. A light filled him, illuminating all the dark corners, chasing out the shadows.

He put a hand on Nate's shoulder. "Sometimes starting over is the best thing."

Nina gave him a curious look and he realized she must have seen a change in him. He bent to kiss her on the forehead, then untied his apron. "There's something I have to take care of. Can you spare me for half an hour?"

"Sure. What's up?"

He headed for the kitchen. "Tell you later," he called out, then hurried out the back door and to the Camry.

On a Sunday, Keith Delacroix would be at home, about a ten-mile drive north of town. Jameson didn't like to bother his former boss on his day off, but Keith's construction firm would be able to provide exactly the services he needed. With the heavy winter rains, Keith's crew had likely been idle more often than not and would appreciate the work.

As he drove to Keith's, he felt something build inside himself, fragile and tentative. For now, he'd let it gain its own strength without forcing himself one way or another. Once the walls were down and he could let the light in, there would be nothing to stop whatever truth lay ahead for him.

That night, it seemed a weight had lifted from Jameson, as if whatever turmoil he'd struggle with had been resolved. The usual dinner rush at the café had been so light they closed an hour early, then picked up a pizza and videos—one a family film, the other a more adult recent release they'd missed in the theater.

They watched the first film with Nate seated between them, sharing a massive bowl of popcorn. After Nate went to bed, Nina cuddled up beside Jameson on the sofa as the second movie started its opening credits. Halfway through, their interest in the film waned as they focused on each other, eager hands and hungry mouths exploring. Nina was half-dressed by the time Jameson carried her to his bedroom, and it didn't take long before they were together in his bed, skin against skin.

Jameson took his time pleasuring her, bringing her to a noisy climax that made her glad two rooms separated their room from Nate's. Once he'd swallowed the last of her cries with his kisses, she rolled him on his back, taking him inside her. She gloried in his release, the way he gave himself over to her. She fell asleep soon after, waking only once when he started another slow tender session of lovemaking. Half-asleep, her body led the way, her arousal leading again to completion.

Lulled back to sleep, it was hours later when a nightmare caught her in its grip. She was in a dark place calling for Nate, but couldn't find him. She stumbled in circles searching for him, calling out his name and Jameson's but no one answered. A sense of dread overwhelmed her.

She woke with a gasp to brilliant sunlight pouring across her face. The house seemed preternaturally quiet, her hammering heartbeat the only sound she heard. She grabbed Jameson's T-shirt from the floor where he'd left it last night, threw it on before hurrying out of the room.

"Jameson? Nate?"

She caught the flicker of flames in the living room fireplace, then continued on to Nate's room. His bed was rumpled, but he was gone. The remnants of the nightmare still with her, an irrational panic burst inside. She rushed back out to check for Jameson's car. The drive was empty. She'd left her little sedan at the café last night, having gone home with Jameson.

They probably just went into town, she told herself, tamping down her ridiculous panic. Maybe to the café to track down that leak in the dishwasher plumbing that Jameson kept promising he'd get to. She'd get dressed, start some coffee, then call the café.

Heading for her own room, Nina pulled on jeans and a sweater and put her hair back in a short ponytail. In the kitchen, she made a quick scan for a note as she started the coffeemaker. No note, no indication of where Jameson and Nate had gone. Anxiety plucked at her, setting up a hundred what-ifs in her mind.

Irritated at her imagination's dark flights of fancy, she picked up the kitchen extension and dialed the café. She listened to it ring until it clicked over to the voice mail, then hung up as the recorded message answered and began to recite their hours of operation.

They'd gone to run some other errand, then. Maybe they went down to Archer's for sweet rolls for breakfast. It was nearly ten o'clock, more than two hours after her early bird son woke, but Jameson could have fed him cereal to tide him over until they could bring home something from the bakery.

She felt a bit foolish calling Archer's to ask if they'd seen Jameson and Nate. But when J.C.'s youngest daughter, Jenna, told Nina they hadn't been in, alarm tickled at her again. She then called Jameson's cell and heard it bleating from his room. He'd left his cell behind.

Her hand trembling, she punched out the number for the Hart Valley Inn. Beth answered on the first ring and after the usual exchange of hellos and how-are-yous, Nina got to the point. "I was wondering if you've seen Jameson and Nate in town today."

"Funny you should ask. Mark said he saw them down in Marbleville earlier this morning. They were headed into the bank."

None of this made sense. Nina said her goodbyes, then set down the phone. After pouring herself a cup of coffee, she wandered back into the living room and stood in front of the fire Jameson had started.

They'd been spending every Monday, their only day off, together as a family for months now. If he'd needed to go into Marbleville for something, why wouldn't he have waited for Nina to wake so she could go with them?

The morning dragged on as she drank too much coffee and stared at CNN on the television without registering any of the world's news. When the phone rang, her heart kicked into overdrive as she raced into the kitchen to answer it. Certain it was her husband calling to explain where he and Nate were, she answered the phone with, "Jameson?"

A long pause, then an unfamiliar male voice asked, "Is Mr. O'Connell in?"

"No, he isn't." Unease dug inside her. "Can I take a message?"

"Mrs. O'Connell?"

"Yes."

"I'm your husband's attorney. He called me with questions about his trust."

"I don't think I can help you." She glanced at the clock—nearly noon. She ought to get off the phone in case Jameson called. "He hasn't told me much about it."

"If you could just relay a message. First, the trust isn't community property. You're unable to access the funds."

Did Jameson want to be sure she couldn't spend the trust money? They hadn't discussed it since that day in San Francisco.

The attorney cleared his throat. "As to the issue of portability—"

"Portability?"

"Mr. O'Connell seemed concerned about ready access if he was no longer in the area. You can let him know he can transfer the trust anywhere he likes."

The attorney gave his phone number, but a roaring in her ears blotted out the man's voice. The phone slipped from her hand.

She raced back to Nate's bedroom and a quick survey told her his backpack was missing, along with his stuffed white tiger and the wooden cars Jameson had given him. She searched his dresser, but couldn't tell what might be gone from the drawers. If Jameson had taken Nate, he wouldn't have to bring anything with him, he could just buy him new with his grandmother's trust.

He wouldn't have, couldn't have taken Nate away from her. She couldn't bring herself to believe that of him. But what had he said the other night, when he'd seemed so troubled? *I wouldn't leave him behind. I couldn't.* Because when he left, he planned to take Nate with him?

Her legs gave way and she crumpled to the floor. She took one breath, another, forcing air into her lungs. She refused to let herself think for the moment, wouldn't allow herself to descend into the abyss of terror that seemed too eager to devour her.

She didn't know how long she huddled there, lost in horror. When she first heard the crunch of tires on gravel, she didn't move, too afraid that if she did, she would make the car go away again. But with the slamming of car doors and Nate's familiar racing footsteps on the porch, she jumped to her feet. She reached the front door just as Nate opened it.

With a cheerful, "Hi, Mommy!" he ran past her down

the hall, hugging his white tiger, his backpack bouncing between his shoulders.

Nina threw herself into Jameson's arms, unmindful of the wind gusting through the still open front door. "I thought you left me."

He pulled her so tightly against her she could barely breath. "No, Nina. God, how could I?"

"You've been acting so strange…then when you were both gone this morning…"

He drew back, and tipped her face up to him. "You thought I would take him from you?"

"I couldn't believe it. Didn't want to." Tears streamed down her face. "But then your attorney called. About the trust."

Reaching behind them, he shut the door. "I wanted to find out if I needed to add your name, and be certain you would have access no matter where you were. Just in case…" He cradled her face with his hands. "Nina, when I first called the attorney…it *was* because I thought about leaving. I kept thinking it would be best…for you, for Nate."

"Jameson." Her hands curled around his wrists, held him tight. "Having you here, that's what's best for me and Nate."

"I'm starting to understand that," he whispered, pressing his forehead to hers. "In any case, I couldn't walk away."

He kissed her, held her so close she felt a part of him. When he pulled back, arms still around her, she saw an unexpected serenity in his face.

"Where did you and Nate go this morning? I didn't see a note."

"I'm such an idiot. I forgot to leave one. Sorry." He pressed a kiss to her brow. "We went to the bank and then Delacroix Construction. I had Nate bring his toys so he wouldn't be bored." He led her to the sofa, tugged her down on his lap. "Afterward, we took a walk. That run-down cabin I grew up in—I own the five acres it sits on. The only thing of value my father left me."

"You were there this morning?"

He nodded. "Nate and I were looking for a place to bury my brother's ashes. I want to start new memories, better memories of that place. Putting my brother to rest there is a start."

Gazing into his eyes, she saw a clarity, an openness she'd never seen before. "I love you, Jameson."

He stroked her cheek. "When you told me you loved me the first time, I was so afraid I would ruin it somehow. If I pushed you away, I would keep it safe."

"There's no way you could ruin my love for you." Her throat tightened. "Even if you never found a way to love me back."

"But I have, Nina." His intense blue eyes softened as he gazed down at her. "I do love you. Desperately. And I want forever with you."

"Forever," she agreed. Holding him close, she welcomed his kiss.

They'd set on this path five years ago, with a heat and passion that had created their son. Now new chances opened up from this moment forward, with hope to gentle the rough terrain, joy to light every dark corner.

And love to turn every day into heaven.

Epilogue

Despite all of Nate's begging, Jameson wouldn't let his son sit in the bulldozer when it brought the old cabin down. Lucky enough for Jameson, he didn't have to be the bad guy—Keith Delacroix firmly informed Nate that Delacroix Construction's insurance didn't cover four-year-olds at the controls of its heavy equipment.

As weak sunlight barely chased the December morning chill, Nate had to satisfy himself with remaining a safe distance away as Keith did his job. As consolation, Jameson gave Nate a disposable camera to record the event as his mother and father looked on. Jameson would just as soon never see the cabin again, even in photographic form, but the pictures would give Nate bragging rights at the preschool. That plus the full-size construction helmet Keith had let him wear distracted the four-year-old from his burning desire to drive a bulldozer.

The rickety structure came down quickly, reduced to

a dusty pile of blackened lumber and broken glass in less than half an hour. Keeping to the perimeter Nina had set, Nate took pictures from every angle, capering around with his camera like a paparazzi in pursuit of a celebrity.

Nina stood at Jameson's side, arm around him, head resting on his shoulder. When he'd told her a week ago about his plan to raze the cabin, she'd agreed it would be a good way to lay his ghosts to rest. When he told her he wanted to donate the land to an organization that provided outdoor experiences for troubled inner city kids, her enthusiasm wiped away any lingering doubts he'd had about the decision.

Now as Keith Delacroix's crew backed the dump truck into position and the skip loader scooped up its first load of shattered lumber and glass, Nina put her arms around him. Reaching up, she kissed him, a soft brushing of lips that teased him with promises of what could come later in the day. Too bad their active four-year-old had given up his afternoon nap.

Nate bounced back to him. "There's no more pictures, Daddy. Can we go home now?" He raced off to the car.

Jameson watched him go. "Was he always so full of energy?"

Nina laughed. "From day one. Ran me ragged."

He sighed. "I'm sorry I missed it."

Her soft smile sent a sweet warmth through him. "But now you have a chance to see babyhood firsthand."

He drew back. "You're not pregnant?"

"Not yet. We've been careful." She tapped his nose. "But I think we ought to try for O'Connell, Part II."

"I like that idea," he said gruffly, his voice clogged with emotion. "What do you say we start trying this afternoon?"

"Absolutely." She glanced over at the car. "I think Nate ought to visit Grandma and Grandpa today, don't you?"

"Oh, yes." Pulling her closer, he poured all his love for her into his kiss. Then, unencumbered by his past, he walked with his beloved wife toward his son and toward his future.

* * * * *

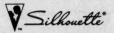

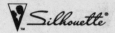

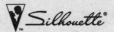

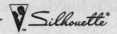

SPECIAL EDITION™

presents
a heartwarming NEW series!

**THE HATHAWAYS
OF MORGAN CREEK:
A DYNASTY
IN THE BAKING...**

NANNY IN HIDING

(SSE #1642, available October 2004)

by

Patricia Kay

On the run from her evil ex-husband, Amy Jordan
accepted blue-eyed Bryce Hathaway's offer to be his
children's nanny. This wealthy single dad was
immediately intrigued by the beautiful runaway, but if
he discovered that this caring, gentle woman was
actually a nanny *in hiding*, would he
help her out—or turn her in?

Available at your favorite retail outlet.

Receive a FREE hardcover book from

HARLEQUIN ROMANCE®

in September!

Harlequin Romance celebrates the launch of
the line's new cover design by offering you
this exclusive offer valid only in September,
only in Harlequin Romance.

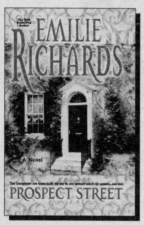

To receive your
FREE HARDCOVER BOOK
written by bestselling author
Emilie Richards, send us four
proofs of purchase from any
September 2004 Harlequin
Romance books. Further details
and proofs of purchase can be
found in all September 2004
Harlequin Romance books.

*Must be postmarked
no later than October 31.*

**Don't forget to be one of the first
to pick up a copy of the new-look
Harlequin Romance novels in September!**

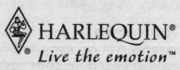

Visit us at www.eHarlequin.com

HRPOP0904

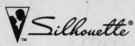

COMING NEXT MONTH

#1639 MARRYING MOLLY—Christine Rimmer
Bravo Family Ties
Salon owner Molly O'Dare vowed to never be single *and* pregnant.
That is, until a passionate love affair landed her in both of these
categories. The child's father—wealthy and dashingly handsome
Tate Bravo—insisted on marrying Molly. But she was determined to
resist until he could offer exactly what she wanted: true love.

#1640 THE PRINCE'S BRIDE—Lois Faye Dyer
The Parks Empire
Wedding planner Emily Parks had long since given up her dream of
starting a family and decided to focus on her career. She never
imagined that the dashing Prince Lazhar Eban would ever want
her to be his bride, but little did she know that what began as a
business proposition would turn into the marriage proposal she'd
always dreamed of!

#1641 THE DEVIL YOU KNOW—Laurie Paige
Seven Devils
When Roni Dalton literally fell onto FBI agent Adam Smith's table
at a restaurant, she set off a chain of mutual passion that neither
could resist. Adam claimed that he was too busy to get involved, but
when he suddenly succumbed to their mutual attraction, Roni was
determined to change this self-proclaimed singleton into a
marriage-minded man.

#1642 NANNY IN HIDING—Patricia Kay
The Hathaways of Morgan Creek
On the run from her evil ex-husband, Amy Jordan accepted blue-
eyed Bryce Hathaway's offer to be his children's nanny. This
wealthy single dad was immediately intrigued by the beautiful
runaway, but if he discovered that this caring, gentle woman was
actually a nanny *in hiding,* would he help her out—or turn her in?

#1643 WRONG TWIN, RIGHT MAN—Laurie Campbell
Beth Montoya and her husband, Rafael, were on the verge of
divorce when Beth barely survived a brutal train accident. When she
was struck with amnesia and mistakenly identified as her
twin sister, Anne, Rafael offered to take care of "Anne" while she
recovered. Suddenly lost passion flared between them…but then her
true identity started to surface.…

#1644 MAKING BABIES—Wendy Warren
Recently divorced Elaine Lowry yearned for a baby of her own.
Enter Mitch Ryder—sinfully handsome and looking for an heir to
carry on his family name. He insisted that their marriage be strictly
business, but what would happen if she couldn't hold up her end of
the deal?

SSECNM0904